"There's not much I'm afraid of."

"Is that so?" Bo touched a hand to her hair. Just a touch, but he saw her smile fade and her eyes go wide. "Is it just me, Kitty? Or do you react to all men this way?"

"What way?"

"You have the same look in your eyes those mustangs had when they heard that gunshot. Like you're about to make a run for it. Why are you running?"

"I'm not…"

It happened so quickly, she had no time to react. His hand closed over her shoulder, holding her when she tried to walk away. In one smooth motion he turned her into his arms. The look in his eyes had her heart leaping to her throat. She had no doubt that he intended to kiss her.

Ruth Langan traces her ancestry to Scotland and Ireland. It is no surprise, then, that she feels a kinship with many of the characters in her historical novels. Married to her childhood sweetheart, she has five children and lives in Michigan, the state where she was born and raised.

Recent titles by the same author:

RORY*
CONOR*
BRIANA*
THE COURTSHIP OF IZZY McCREE
BADLANDS LAW†
BADLANDS LEGEND†

*The O'Neil Saga
†The Badlands

BADLANDS
HEART

Ruth Langan

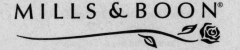

MILLS & BOON®

All the characters in this book have no existence outside the imagination of the author, and have no relation whatsoever to anyone bearing the same name or names. They are not even distantly inspired by any individual known or unknown to the author, and all the incidents are pure invention.

First published in Great Britain 2005
Harlequin Mills & Boon Limited,
Eton House, 18-24 Paradise Road, Richmond, Surrey TW9 1SR

© Ruth Ryan Langan 2002

ISBN 0 263 84366 1

Set in Times Roman 10½ on 13 pt.
04-0405-58202

Printed and bound in Spain
by Litografia Rosés S.A., Barcelona

For our very own Kitty Stone.

And of course for Tom
Always

Prologue

Dakota Territory—1867

The little party of mourners stood on a sun-baked hill, sweltering under a relentless haze of heat that rivaled the fires of hell. There had been no rain for weeks, and the scorched earth had begun to split and crack. The silence was broken by the distant rumble of thunder, but the ranchers of the Dakota Territory had given up looking to the heavens. Instead, they felt the ground under their feet shudder, and knew it was a herd of buffalo, thundering across the plains in search of precious prairie grass.

At the gravesite of her grandfather, a bewildered five-year-old Kitty Conover stood between her two brothers, ten-year-old Gabriel and nine-year-old Yale. The three watched as half a dozen neighbors took turns tossing a handful of dirt on the wooden box. It was the first time Kitty had ever seen her two brothers in suits. Her ma had been up all night sewing for them. Dorry Conover said she did it out of respect for their grandpa. After all, Deacon Conover, their father's father, a stern bear of a man, had taken them in when they'd had nowhere else to go.

Whenever her children asked about their father, Dorry told them proudly that after he'd finished soldiering in the Great War, Clay Conover had been sent on a secret assignment that had been authorized by President Lincoln himself before his untimely assassination.

Kitty didn't understand what that meant. Nor did she understand what they were doing here today. All she wanted was to go back home, so her ma wouldn't look unhappy, and Gabe wouldn't look uncomfortable, and Yale could resume teasing her the way he always did.

Seeing her start to rub her eyes, Yale poked an elbow into her arm and whispered that he was going to toss her into the grave with their grandpa. She opened her mouth to let out a yelp. Before she could make a sound, Gabriel glanced over and, seeing his uncle Junior's withering look, picked her up and held her until the gaping hole was filled.

As the neighboring ranchers returned to their wagons, Dorry called out, ''You're all welcome to come back to our place for supper. I killed a couple of chickens. They're simmering in a pot right now.''

Several of their neighbors seemed about to agree until, seeing the scowl on her brother-in-law's face, they offered their apologies and hastened back to their own ranches.

As Dorry was climbing into her wagon Junior caught her roughly by the arm, stopping her in mid-step. ''What right have you got inviting them back to eat my food?''

Dorry seemed genuinely surprised by his outburst and tried to lower her voice. ''Junior, these are your neighbors. They came all this way just to pay their last respects to your father. Some of them will be on the trail for hours before they get home. It's only right that we offer them our hospitality.''

''Oh, you'd be good at that, wouldn't you? You know all about accepting hospitality.''

At her uncle's outburst, Kitty, who had just been lifted into the back of the wagon by Gabriel, turned around in surprise.

Dorry's voice took on that quiet, respectful tone she'd learned to use around her husband's older brother whenever he was on one of his tirades. ''What are you talking about, Junior?''

''I'm not Junior anymore.'' His voice seemed as hot as the sun. As hard as the baked earth. ''I've always hated that name. With the old man gone, I'm Deacon now. Deacon Conover. And don't you forget it.''

Dorry nodded. ''Whatever you say.''

''That's right.'' He glanced at the mound of dirt, then back at her, his face hard and tight with fury. ''It's whatever I say now. Not the old man. I told him he was a fool to take on four more mouths. But you fed him that lie about Clay, and he swallowed it whole.''

''Lie? What are you…?'' She glanced toward the back of the wagon and could see her three children watching and listening in horrified fascination.

''That pretty little sugarcoated story about Clay carrying on some secret mission for the president. You and the old man both knew it was a lie. Clay's never coming back for you.'' His voice lifted to a whine. ''You could have had yourself a solid, dependable husband, Dorry. You knew I wanted you. When we were kids, you were just about the prettiest girl around. With all that yellow hair and those big blue eyes.''

Over Gabriel's shoulder Kitty stared at her mother, trying to see her through her uncle's eyes. Was Ma pretty? She'd never thought about it. All she knew was that she worked from sunup to sundown, just to keep her family fed and clothed.

Junior's tone hardened. ''But you just had to go and give your heart to my reckless little brother. And look what it got you. Three brats, and a husband who left you to run off with the most dangerous gang of outlaws in the land.''

From the back of the wagon Kitty gave out a startled cry. At once Gabriel drew her into his arms, pressing his hands over her ears, even though he knew it was too late. She'd heard. They'd all heard those cruel, cutting words. Words that had struck with all the force of a blow to the heart.

An outlaw? Her pa, an outlaw? Kitty struggled to deny it. It wasn't possible. Still, now that the word had been spoken aloud, it seemed to make sense to the little girl. After all, her father was little more than a stranger. A man in a soldier's uniform who rode off to fight, and except for brief periods, was rarely seen again. Was that why Pa had left them? To join a gang of outlaws?

For the space of a heartbeat Dorry seemed frozen to the spot, unable to speak. Unable to move. Finally she drew in a long breath. ''You'll be burdened with us no longer. We'll stay only long enough to fetch our things. Then we'll be through accepting your hospitality.''

She climbed up to the wagon and flicked the reins. As they started across the hills, nobody spoke. Neither the woman who drove the team, the children seated in the back of the wagon, nor the man who rode his horse in stone-faced silence alongside them.

At the ranch Dorry moved from room to room, bundling up their meager belongings, supervising as Gabriel and Yale secured them in the back of the wagon. She took Kitty with her as she walked the garden, taking care to pick only half the rain-starved crop, leaving the other half for her brother-in-law. She did the same with the chickens, tossing half a dozen in a pen, along with a rooster. She tied a young cow behind the wagon, then ordered her children to climb aboard.

Junior stood in the doorway, grinning foolishly. "You want me to beg, don't you, Dorry? That's what this is about, isn't it?"

She said nothing as she picked up the reins.

His smile faded as he ran down the steps and started racing alongside. "All right. I'm sorry for what I said back there, Dorry. But the brats had to hear it sometime. Besides, you know you can't really leave. Where will you go?"

She reined in the horse long enough to say, "I'm heading for the Badlands. That's where Clay said he'd be. As for you, I never want to see you again, Junior." And then, because she'd been pushed to the limit, she added, "You'll never be Deacon Conover to me, Junior. You're not half the man your father was. Or your brother, Clay."

She urged the horse into a trot, leaving her brother-in-law standing in the dust, staring after her.

Kitty Conover watched her mother's lips tremble, even as she held her head high. And though her two brothers stared straight ahead, she turned back to watch as her grandfather's ranch faded into the distance.

It was the only home she'd ever known. And now it was gone. Like her pa. Like her grandpa.

She hunkered down into the back of the wagon and wondered, as only a child can, if she'd ever have a home, or a family, again.

In the days that followed, their little odyssey became a test of endurance. To spare their horse, the family walked as much as possible until, drained by heat and exhaustion, they would make camp during the hottest part of the day and begin walking again after sundown. To keep their minds off their fears, their mother passed the time telling them tales of her childhood in Missouri, or coaching them in spelling and sums.

''You owe it to me and your pa to make something of your lives, children. You can't ever let life's trials beat you down.''

''Yes'm.'' It was most often Gabriel who answered for all of them, for he could see what this journey was doing to their mother. Every day, every mile, seemed to sap her energy, until, within weeks, she was going on pure will.

By the time they left the muddy Missouri River behind and headed west, toward the deep canyons and steep mountains that the Sioux called *mako sica,* meaning bad land, the hens had stopped laying and they'd been forced to kill them for food. Days later the cow dried up and they slaughtered her, as well, rationing the meat for the hard times ahead.

Their family witnessed a variety of bewildering extremes. There seemed to be limitless expanses of space, but almost no people. They traversed sweeping treeless plains and steep, forested mountains, but spent hours searching in vain for water.

To Kitty, each day seemed to bring something new and challenging. But when Dorry Conover awoke one morning with a raging fever that gradually grew worse, Kitty faced the greatest challenge of her young life.

"You ride in the wagon with Kitty, Ma." Gabe helped her into the back and laid her down among the quilts, then took up the reins and began walking.

Kitty, who sat squeezing her mother's hand, could overhear her two brothers.

Yale turned to Gabriel. "What if Ma dies?"

Gabriel grabbed him by the throat, his eyes hot with fury. "She isn't going to die."

Yale shoved his hand away and lifted a fist, ready to stand and fight. "Who says? People die, Gabe. Gramps died, didn't he?"

"That was different. Gramps was old."

"Young people die, too. Remember Pa's friends who died in the war?"

"That was war. This is…" He shook his head, struggling to find a word to describe the hell they were in.

"This is a different kind of war, Gabe." Because he was scared, Yale lowered his voice. "It's just us against the Badlands. But it's war all the same."

The two brothers fell silent, each lost in their own terrible thoughts, unaware that their words had left their little sister feeling too numb to speak, or even to weep.

By the time they stopped for the night Dorry was too weak to sit up. She clutched their hands and struggled to make herself understood.

"Your pa's a good man. An honorable man. Don't believe what your uncle said about him."

Gabriel spoke for all of them. "We know, Ma. You just rest and get your strength back."

She shook her head. "I'm not going to be with you. I can feel my strength ebbing. But I want you to know that my spirit will always be with you. Don't be afraid. You have your father's blood flowing through you. That Conover blood will make you strong enough to prevail over anything." She squeezed Gabriel's hand, and turned to look at her middle child, Yale, and then at her baby, Kitty, as though memorizing their faces. "You take care of each other, you hear me?"

"Yes'm." Gabriel nudged his brother and sister, and the two answered in kind.

Even as they were speaking, Kitty saw her mother's hand slip from Gabe's. Saw the way her eyes went sightless. And knew, in that one terrible moment, that her mother was gone.

They left the crude grave with its simple stone marker at first light and started out. Kitty lagged behind, staring tearfully at the spot where her mother lay. Her tears were as much from anger as sadness. What would happen to them now? Would they still be a family?

Seeing the tears she couldn't hide, Yale knelt down and hauled her onto his back, pretending to be her horse until he had her giggling as he trotted up a hill.

They made camp that night by a mud hole that had once been a stream. Still, though the water tasted foul, Gabe boiled it over the fire and when it had cooled, passed it around.

In the morning when Kitty awoke, she saw Yale striding toward them, his face wreathed in smiles.

"Where've you been?" At the sound of Gabe's voice Kitty turned to her oldest brother. His features were tight with anger. She sensed instinctively that beneath the anger lay a deep well of fear.

"Getting us some supplies." Yale held up a jug and uncorked it, filling a tin cup with milk. He passed it to Kitty and she drank it down in long gulps.

Gabe's tone lowered "Where'd you find milk out here?"

Kitty turned from one brother to the other, her eyes wide and wise.

"There's a ranch about a mile from here."

"And the rancher gave you milk and supplies?"

"In a way." Yale's grin widened. "'Course, he doesn't know it yet. And I'd advise us to be long gone before he finds his prize calf slaughtered." He tossed a hunk of raw meat, as much as he'd been able to carry, in the back of the wagon and covered it with a blanket to hide the evidence.

"You stole his milk and butchered his calf?" Gabe looked horrified.

"That's right." Yale pushed him aside and lifted Kitty into the back of the wagon. "Now let's get. It'll be light soon."

They managed to cross a muddy creek and pass through a forest before making camp. But that night, for the first time in weeks, they went to bed with their stomachs full.

Before she drifted off to sleep Kitty lay between

her brothers, warmed by the heat of their bodies, lulled by the sound of their soft, even breathing.

Maybe it didn't matter so much if their pa was an outlaw, and their ma was lying in a grave, as long as they stuck together. But what would she do if anything happened to Gabe and Yale? What if their constant bickering over who was right and who wrong drove a wedge between them, driving them apart?

She knew, with the wisdom of a woman-child, that it would be up to her to find a way to keep them together. They were, after all, the only thing that mattered to her. Family.

Two weeks later, when they'd gone through the last of their meat, they came up over a rise and saw a small encampment of wagons and shacks. As they drew near they saw an old man tending a herd of cows. He looked up as their little party approached.

"'Afternoon, children. Welcome to Misery.''

It was Gabe who spoke. ''Misery?''

Seeing their surprise the old man laughed, showing a gaping hole where his teeth had once been. ''That's the name of our little place. We figure we're all sharing in it together. My name's Aaron Smiler.''

Gabe offered a handshake. ''I'm Gabriel Conover. This is my brother, Yale.'' He pointed to the back of the wagon. ''And that's our little sister, Kitty.''

At the sight of the little girl the old man touched

a gnarled hand to his wide-brimmed hat in a courtly gesture that warmed her heart. ''Where're your folks?''

''Our ma's buried along the trail. We're heading for the Badlands to join up with our pa.'' Gabe looked at the old man hopefully. ''You wouldn't happen to know him, would you? Clay Conover.''

The old man shook his head. ''Sorry, son. Never heard of him.'' He glanced at the weary little party before pointing toward a rough shack in the distance. ''That's my place. Why don't you stop awhile and I'll make you some vittles.''

At that Kitty perked up considerably.

Gabe held back. ''We can't pay you, Mr. Smiler.''

''Well, now. Maybe you could lend a hand with some of the chores around here. I'm getting on in years, and I can't do all the things I used to.''

All three children nodded in agreement.

''All right, then.'' The old man led the way. ''Maybe, if you decide you like it here, you'll make Misery your home for a while. Just until you're ready to resume your search for your pa, that is.''

''Thank you, Mr. Smiler.''

At her brother's words, Kitty felt a strange flutter in the pit of her stomach. For now, for as long as the old man would have them, they'd found a place to settle. To stay together.

It was all Kitty yearned for in her heart of hearts.

To be strong, like her brothers. And to remain together, no matter how many differences were between them.

To be, for now, for all time, a family.

Chapter One

Dakota Territory—1888

"There you are. I've got you now." Kitty Conover peered over the top of a grassy hill and smiled
at the sight of the herd of mustangs below.

Dressed in buckskins, yellow curls tucked under
a wide-brimmed hat, Kitty was a familiar figure
around the little town of Misery. She'd been known
to follow a herd of mustangs for weeks if necessary,
until she captured them and brought them back to
the ranch she shared with Aaron Smiler, the man
who had raised her.

By breaking mustangs to saddle, and selling them
to nearby ranchers, or occasionally to the U.S. Army,
she was able to eke out a living for herself and the
old man who had opened his home to three weary
orphans over twenty years ago.

She'd been on the trail of this herd for six days now. It was one of the biggest yet, with more than three dozen mares, at least a dozen of which were heavy with unborn foals, and a fine spotted stallion, who'd led her on a merry chase.

"Think you're smarter than me, don't you, old Spot?" She noted the end of the box canyon, walled in with high, sheer rock. There was only one way out, and she intended to be there waiting with lasso ready when the herd tried to leave.

She was just about to turn away when a shot rang out. The stallion suddenly reared up and let loose with a warning whinny to the mares. For a moment there was complete chaos as the horses began wheeling and running, eyes wide, nostrils flared, snorting in fear.

Kitty turned back, straining to see through the blur of horses' bodies and the clouds of dust churned up by their hooves.

Was that a man kneeling in the dirt?

"Oh, no, you don't. You miserable, no-good flea-bitten, lop-eared son of a she-bear." She continued in a litany of furious oaths that would curl most men's hair as she started down the hill in a dead run. "You're not stealing my mustangs. Not after all the blood and sweat I've put into this herd."

She made a flying leap into the saddle and used her knees to start her mare into a gallop as she uncoiled her lasso. She hadn't lost them yet. If she could manage to capture the stallion, the mares would follow behind.

Horse and rider came across the steep slope at a run and rounded a bend just as the herd raced past them. Mingled with the herd were several men on horseback. None of them seemed concerned with keeping up with the mustangs, but rather with getting out of their way. As they veered off, they were swallowed up by the cloud of dust.

Kitty braced herself, knowing she had only one slim chance to catch the stallion now. She'd originally planned to have several ropes strung across the narrow entrance, holding the herd inside the box canyon while she captured their leader. Now they were dancing by in a cloud of blinding dust and thundering hooves.

As the stallion drew near she realized the hopelessness of the situation. He'd been thoroughly spooked. From the wild look in his eyes, she knew he'd be more than willing to drag her across a hundred miles of wilderness before he'd even slow his pace.

As the last of the herd raced by, she was forced to put away her lasso. Pulling her rifle from the boot of her saddle, she urged her mare into the box canyon, determined to give this remaining cowboy a piece of her mind.

Spotting him near a rock, she dropped from the saddle and took aim with her rifle. "Quit hiding behind that rock, you useless piece of cow dung, and face me like a man."

When there was no reply she stepped closer. "You think I can't see you?" She gave his boot a vicious kick. "You just cost me the best herd of mustangs I've found all spring. Now you're going to apologize, you no-good, shriveled-up..."

She heard a moan. Low and deep and filled with pain. In that instant her expression changed. Though she kept her rifle ready, in case it was a trick, she stepped around the rock.

A man was lying in the dirt, both hands pressed to his chest. Blood spilled through his fingers and soaked the front of his coat, before running in a river to form a mottled red pool beside him.

Now Kitty understood why those horsemen were so eager to escape, they would even brave a herd of nervous mustangs. It had been their gunfire that had started that stampede.

She tossed aside her rifle and reached for the knife at her belt. There was no time to waste. She would have to locate the wound, determine if there was a bullet, and do what was necessary, if this stranger hoped to see another sunrise.

Kitty struck her flint, coaxing a thin flame in the kindling. Soon the pile of logs was ablaze, and the air was filled with the fragrance of boiling coffee.

She leaned her back against her saddle and glanced up at the stars. She'd hoped to be home by now, snug in her bed in the loft of Aaron Smiler's cabin. She worried over Aaron when she was gone too long. He was getting on in years, and his leg pained him too much to allow for many chores. Most days the old man was content to sit on the porch, watching while she broke her mustangs to saddle. Now he'd be forced to spend another night alone.

Alone. The very word had the power to make her shiver.

She glanced over at the man asleep in her bedroll, wondering if he had family somewhere. If so they'd be worrying over him. Wondering when he was coming home.

It appeared that he'd been shot with a pistol, not a rifle. She'd managed to remove the bullet and had used the whiskey she'd found in his saddlebags to disinfect the wound before binding it. Now he lay in a deep sleep, neither moving, nor even moaning. But his breathing, though shallow, was steady enough. As was his heartbeat.

She helped herself to some dried meat from her saddlebags and filled a tin cup with steaming coffee, glancing idly at the blood that stained the front of her buckskin shirt. This day certainly hadn't turned out as she'd planned. Not that she minded another night under the stars. She felt as comfortable here in this canyon as she would in her own bed. This wild, primitive countryside was her friend. She knew every odd-shaped rock, every mountain peak, every bend in the trail. As for surprises, she'd learned years ago to expect the unexpected and ride them to their conclusion.

She tossed aside the last of the foul-tasting coffee before wrapping herself in her cowhide jacket and pulling her hat over her face. She was asleep almost at once.

It wasn't so much a sound that awakened Kitty; it was more a feeling. She knew instinctively that someone was watching her. She sat up and found the man's eyes fixed on her with a look of confusion.

"You're awake." She tossed aside her cowhide jacket and scrambled to her feet. Kneeling beside him she touched a hand to his forehead. "Your fever's down. Any pain?"

"Yeah." He was still studying her in a quiet, watchful way that put her in mind of a mountain cat. Not so much questioning as assessing.

"This ought to help some." She reached for the whiskey and uncorked it, then lifted his head and held the jug to his mouth.

He took a long pull before she lowered it and set it aside.

He winced as he wiped the back of his hand over his mouth. Even that small movement sent pain crashing through him. ''Thanks. Who are you?''

''Name's Kitty. Kitty Conover. What's yours?''

''Bo Chandler.''

''Who shot you, Bo Chandler?''

He shrugged, then had to fight the quick jolt of pain. ''I don't know. Three men, I think. I'm not sure. Wanted my horse, I guess.'' He glanced over at his bloody jacket and shirt which lay in a heap beside him. ''Did they empty my pockets?''

''I wouldn't know.''

He looked up at her in surprise. ''You never checked?''

She shook her head. ''I figured if you died, I'd have to find out who you were to notify any kin. But since you were still alive, it seemed none of my business.'' She reached for the jacket and felt in the pockets, finding them empty. ''Sorry. Looks like they cleaned you out.''

He nodded. ''I guess I'd expected as much.''

She walked to the fire and added more wood before setting the blackened coffeepot over the flame. A short time later she handed him a steaming cup of coffee. ''This won't taste like much, but it might warm you up some.''

"Thanks." He winced again as he sat up, causing the blankets to slide to his waist.

Kitty turned away and retrieved her saddle, then crossed to him and placed it behind his back for support. As she did, she became aware of the fact that he was naked to the waist.

Last night she'd been concerned only with saving his life, as she'd stripped away his shirt and coat before cutting into his flesh. Now it was impossible to ignore the way the muscles of his arms bunched and flexed as he lifted the cup to his lips. Or to ignore the width of his shoulders. Or the flat, narrow planes of his hair-roughened chest and stomach.

Even in his weakened state, there was something dark and dangerous about him. His face was lean. Black hair curled over his forehead. His eyes were gray and full of shadows. A stubble of growth darkened his chin and cheeks, but not enough to hide a firm, chiseled jaw.

He managed a few sips of coffee before slumping forward without making a sound. As he did, the cup slipped from his nerveless fingers.

Kitty felt for his pulse. Relieved that it was strong and steady, she covered him with the blankets, then went off in search of game. It looked as though they wouldn't be leaving this place anytime soon.

A wound like that might have killed a lesser man. But Bo Chandler was a fighter.

She liked that in a man.

"How long have I been out?" Bo's words were slurred from a mixture of pain and sleep.

"All of yesterday and the night before." Kitty yawned and stretched before looking up at the stars. She'd been having such a nice dream. Her ma had been at a big wooden table, serving up chicken for her family. Not that she had actually seen her. Kitty had long ago forgotten her mother's face. But she knew it was her ma all the same. There had been a cozy fire on the hearth, and flowers in a glass vase on the windowsill. And cows lowing out in the field. Even now, with the dream fading, there was still a feeling of love and peace in her heart. "You in pain?"

"Yeah."

"I'll fetch you some whiskey." Kitty knelt beside him. As before, she lifted his head and held the jug to his mouth. "Good thing you'd already removed your saddlebags or we wouldn't even have this."

"I was going to make camp here and watch the herd of mustangs. I'd just turned away when I heard the gunshot and felt the pain of the bullet. I never even saw them coming."

He drank several long swallows before refusing more. "What's that I smell? Venison?"

"I killed a deer." She corked the jug, then poured

some liquid into a cup. "I made you some broth from the innards."

She waited until he'd managed to sit up before handing it to him, then watched as he sipped and swallowed.

From the look on his face she couldn't tell if he was surprised or angry.

His tone was rough. "Are you trying to poison me?"

"I thought it might give you some strength."

"You mean, if it didn't kill me first."

Instead of taking offense, she merely laughed. "Like Aaron says, I'm not much for cooking. But I can keep body and soul together."

"Who's Aaron? Your husband?"

That brought more laughter. "Aaron's sort of like my grandfather, I guess."

"What's that supposed to mean?"

"I live on Aaron's ranch. And share his home."

"So you cook and clean for him?"

Still chuckling, she carved off several slices of deer meat from the carcass roasting over the fire and handed him a plate. "You've tasted my cooking. My cleaning's not much better. Neither of us cares much for household chores, so we do what we have to and ignore the rest. Aaron's pretty lame now, so he can't do much anymore. I earn enough for both of us by breaking mustangs to saddle and selling or bartering them for whatever we need.''

That would explain the buckskins, he thought as he forced down several bites of deer meat before sipping the foul-tasting broth.

A short time later he glanced at the jug. ''I'd like more whiskey now.''

When she held it to his lips he couldn't decide if he'd asked for it to wash away the taste of her cooking, or because of the quick jolt of pleasure he got whenever she cradled his head in her arms.

She bent forward slightly, causing a strand of her hair to brush his cheek. It was as soft as a snowflake.

As she tucked the blankets around him, he breathed her in. She smelled like a woman, he realized, something he hadn't experienced in some time. But not like a saloon woman. More like a creature of the wild. As fresh as a clear mountain stream. With just a hint of evergreen clinging to her hair and clothing.

What a strange woman. She might not be able to cook, but she'd done a damned fine job on his wound. Though it burned like the fire of hell, he could see that it was free of infection. She didn't seem at all concerned about spending her nights in this wilderness, without any of the comforts most women would demand. She'd killed a deer, skinned and cooked it. And though she dressed like some sort of wild mountain creature, her speech told him she'd had at least a little education.

She intrigued him.

Despite the pain he drifted back to sleep with a smile on his lips.

Chapter Two

"Sorry." Bo opened his eyes to see Kitty dragging tree branches down the side of the hill and spreading them like a roof between several big boulders. "It seems that all I do is lie here and apologize for being so useless. How long have I been asleep this time?"

"Most of the afternoon. But don't worry about it. Sleep's necessary for healing, according to Aaron."

He started to sit up and sucked in a breath at the blaze of searing pain. "If that's true, why isn't it working for me?"

She paused in her work to smile. "You're a lot better than you were yesterday. I figure another day or two and you'll be strong enough to sit on a horse."

"I hope you're right." He nodded toward the shelter she was building. "What's that for?"

She pointed skyward. "Storm clouds up there. We'll be a lot more comfortable out of the rain."

"You think a few branches will keep us dry?"

"They will if they're lined with a fresh deer skin." Without seeming to hurry she moved efficiently around the campfire, cutting the deer meat into small chunks before stashing them in a corner of the shelter along with her cowhide jacket and saddlebags.

She paused beside him. "Think you can walk that far with my help?"

"I can try." He accepted her outstretched hands and pulled himself up, struggling not to give in to the pain that threatened to overwhelm him.

He was surprised at how small she was. From his position in the bedroll, he'd watched her do the work of a man without any seeming effort. There was a feeling of such strength about her that he was caught by surprise when he realized her head barely reached his chin.

Kitty draped his arm around her shoulder and took a firm hold at his waist. That was her first mistake. The feel of that warm, naked flesh against her palm had her pulling her hand away as though burned. Then, to cover her awkwardness, she forced herself to take hold of him again and attempt a step. Another mistake, she realized. For he was leaning on her in such a way she felt completely off balance. Her head was actually spinning, and she had to grit her teeth to keep going.

He gave a grunt of pain. "Now I know how a baby feels when he tries walking upright."

She tried to laugh, but the sound came out on a hiss of breath. "Just don't fall, or you'll take us both down."

"I'm trying not…" He turned his head to speak and found his lips pressed to her hair. The rush of heat that spiraled through him had him sweating.

At his silence she looked up in alarm. "Are you all right?"

"I'm…" For the space of a heartbeat his thoughts were so jumbled, he couldn't even remember his name. Then, to cover, he managed to mumble, "I'm fine. I'll make it."

"Just a few more steps." She hoped. If she didn't soon let go of him and make her escape, she was afraid the heat of his body might burn a hole clean through her hand.

When they reached the shelter he ducked his head and stumbled forward. If it wasn't for her strong, steady grasp, he'd have pitched facedown. Instead he managed to sink to the ground, where he sat breathing heavily while she hurried away to retrieve the bedroll.

Kitty was grateful for the chance to catch her breath. What was happening to her? She was a calm, sensible woman who'd seen half-naked men on hundreds of occasions. Anyone with two brothers as bold as Gabe and Yale should have no qualms about seeing a man in all manner of undress. But there was just something about this man that had her reacting in a whole new way. A way she didn't much care for. She was reminded of those silly girls in Misery who used to blush and giggle whenever Gabe and Yale would go into town. She'd never understood such behavior. Now she was doing practically the same thing, and it bothered her more than she cared to admit.

She refused to dwell on it. Instead, she plunged herself into the work at hand, tossing the bedroll over her arm, hauling it back to the shelter, then laying it out, before turning away.

"Think you can manage by yourself?" She heard the breathiness in her tone and blamed it on the fact that she was racing the storm. Still, she was determined not to touch him again.

"Sure. I'm fine." Bo studied her retreating back before attempting to struggle his way into the bedroll.

He lay panting while she finished a quick sweep of their campsite. She was, he thought, like a little whirlwind of activity, tethering the horse, tossing the saddle over her shoulder, then, as an afterthought, pausing to retrieve the blackened pot of coffee from the fire.

No sooner had she returned to the shelter than the first raindrops began falling. Within minutes it became a downpour.

Kitty filled a tin cup with steaming coffee and handed it to Bo. ''Where are you from?''

''Here and there.'' He drank, then passed it back to her to share.

''You don't look like a drifter.'' She thought about the clothes she'd had to cut through to get at his wound. And the crisp white shirt in his saddlebag. ''In these parts most drifters don't wear white shirts and fancy dark coats.''

''I didn't say I was a drifter. But I've been to a lot of places.''

''Such as?''

He thought a minute. ''I've been east, to Boston and New York. Traveled most of the South. Atlanta, Charleston. And I've been as far west as California.''

Her head was spinning from the thought of seeing all those places. ''I've never been anywhere except Misery.''

''What's Misery?''

''A town just beyond the Badlands.''

''Were you born there?''

She shook her head. ''I've been told I was born

in a wagon heading from Missouri to my grandpa's farm in the Dakota Territory.'' She looked over at Bo. ''Where were you born?''

''Virginia.'' He said the word softly, the way a man would speak of a lover.

''What's it like in Virginia?''

He linked his arms behind his head. ''Rolling green hills. Meadows filled with wildflowers in summer. And some of the finest horseflesh in the country.''

''Finer than our mustangs?''

''They're very different. The mustangs are wild, so they've adapted to surviving in the wilderness. The Virginia horses have been carefully bred, so they're sleek and strong and fast.''

''Not as fast as our mustangs, I'd wager.''

''In the short run, the Thoroughbred would win. But for distance the mustangs have it all over the Thoroughbreds.''

''Really?'' Intrigued, she sat up, her eyes animated. ''Is that what your family does? Raise horses?''

''They did.'' His voice lowered. ''Before the war, my grandfather had one of the finest horse farms in Virginia. Afterward, my father kept one or two of the mares for breeding, and tried his hand as a gentleman farmer. But it was never the same after the war.''

Kitty thought of the war that had taken her father away. And the mystery that had surrounded his absence from their family afterward. It seemed so long ago now.

Bo's voice broke into her thoughts. "You never told me how you happened to find me way out here."

"I was trailing a herd of mustangs. I just about had them, too, when that gunshot spooked them."

"I saw them, before I was shot. In fact, that's how I happened to get too distracted to see my attackers sneaking up on me. I was busy admiring the herd. It looked like a pretty good size."

She nodded. "The biggest one yet."

"Then I'm sorry you couldn't go after them."

"That's all right. A herd that big is bound to leave tracks. I'll come across them again. And next time, that old spotted stallion won't get away from me."

Despite his pain Bo managed a smile. "I'd put my money on you any time."

"Thanks." She picked up a hunk of venison. "Care for some supper?"

He shook his head. "Not yet." He'd been quick to learn that if he waited until he was near starvation, Kitty's cooking went down easier.

Not that he could fault her. She'd had little enough to work with. A gun and knife, a deer and a fire. He considered himself lucky to have fallen into her capable hands. Left on his own, he'd have surely bled to death.

He studied her profile, wondering how someone who looked so fragile and pretty could be so tough. "I hate to think what would have happened to me if you hadn't been here."

"I just wish I'd known those cowboys had shot you. I might have been able to pick off one or two of them before they got clean away. When I saw them racing past with the herd, I figured their only crime was stealing my mustangs. Not worth shooting a man for."

"Why didn't you go after them?"

"A couple of reasons. First, because I've seen how long and how far a band of wild horses is able to run when they're spooked. I figured nobody was going to catch them, least of all those cowboys. Second, I'm no fool. I'm not about to pick a fight with three armed men without a good reason."

Bo grinned. "Why do I have the feeling that you wouldn't back down, even if your opponents had you twice as outnumbered?"

Kitty leaned her back against her saddle and drew her cowhide jacket around her shoulders to ward off the growing chill. "I've had to stand my ground a time or two when the odds weren't in my favor. And I'm proud of the fact that I'm still standing. But it's not something I'd choose to do."

"I guess nobody would."

She nodded toward the pistol in his gun belt, lying atop his bloody shirt and jacket. "You know how to use that?"

"Why do you ask?"

She shrugged, and felt the heat rise to her cheeks. She'd noted the softness of his hands. This was no cowboy. Still, he didn't look like a gambler, either. There was none of the polished smoothness of her brother, Yale, who had spent the best part of his youth challenging gamblers in saloons and pleasure palaces. "Those cowboys could decide to come back. I'd like to know I wouldn't have to face them alone."

His tone hardened. "Don't worry. If they come back, you won't have to face them at all. I'll be more than happy to deal with them myself."

She heard the thread of steel in his voice, and saw the way his eyes narrowed. It occurred to her that her first impression of him had been right. Despite the soft hands and fancy clothes, there was something dark and dangerous about Bo Chandler. Something just a little mysterious.

Each of them grew silent, lost in their own thoughts. As darkness overtook the land; they lay listening to the rain.

The sound of it soon lulled them both to sleep.

Hours later Kitty awoke to find herself snuggled

inside the folds of a blanket. She sighed in contentment and rolled to one side, only to find her cheek
buried against the warmth of a muscled chest. The
strong, steady beat of a heart matched the sound of
raindrops falling just beyond the shelter.

As realization dawned, she froze.

How had this happened? Before she'd fallen
asleep, there had been the width of her saddle between her and Bo. Somehow she'd gravitated toward
the warmth of her bedroll. Or possibly toward the
warmth of his body.

For whatever reason, she was now in a horribly
awkward situation. She had to find a way to extricate
herself without waking him.

Lifting the edge of the blanket, she started to ease
away. Just then he sighed and tossed a leg over hers.
To make matters worse, his arm came around her,
pinning her firmly against the length of him.

She lay perfectly still, her heart slamming against
her ribs. Should she simply push away and risk waking him? Or should she outwait him, hoping he
might move again, freeing her?

"Comfortable?" The deep voice, spoken against
her temple, seemed to vibrate all through her system,
sending icicles dancing down her spine.

"You're awake?" She struggled to push free and
found herself being held in an iron grasp. "How
long have you known?"

"Just long enough to realize I'm enjoying this. Especially with all that wiggling going on. Do you have any idea what that's doing to me?"

She could feel the heat rush to her cheeks. It matched the heat that had replaced the ice along her spine. In fact, her entire body felt on fire. "Let me go, you miserable, dog-eared, flea-bitten son of a she-bear."

The richness and variety of her curses had him grinning. "And miss all this fun?"

"You're the one who's going to be missing something if you don't let me go right this minute."

Bo felt the press of her pistol against his thigh. He wisely lifted his hands. "Now there's one order I have no intention of arguing with."

As she scrambled out of the bedroll he added, "You're going to miss my warm body over there on that side of the shelter, Kitty."

"If you're not careful, that warm body of yours will be a dead one."

"Yes, ma'am." His smile grew. His voice was warm with the laughter he was struggling to keep under control. "Just remember. If you should get cold during the night, I'm more than happy to share. After all, it is your bedroll."

She could see the grin on his face, which only added to her embarrassment. She turned away to hide the flush she knew he could see on her cheeks.

As she gathered her cowhide jacket around her, she realized the night had grown bitterly cold. The wind had the bite of a razor's edge.

No matter.

She'd freeze into a block of solid ice before she'd let him see how miserable she felt.

Chapter Three

Bo awoke and lay quietly for a moment, knowing that any movement would bring pain. A glance around the shelter told him Kitty was already up and gone. A pity. He'd have enjoyed watching her a bit more while she slept. When she was awake she was so alive. So animated. But last night, when he'd realized she was lying beside him, he'd been pleasantly surprised by the change he could sense in her while sleeping. That small, heart-shaped face in repose had reminded him of an angel. A sprightly, innocent cherub. Those full pouty lips had been softly curved in a smile, as though enjoying a happy dream. Those pale lashes cast shadows on skin that was like fine porcelain.

It had been an absolute delight to watch her trying to quietly extricate herself from an embarrassing situation. And when she'd come to the realization that he was witnessing what she was going through, her temper had been equally glorious to see. She had a fascinating vocabulary when she swore. At least he assumed she was swearing, though none of the oaths she used were any he'd heard before.

What a fascinating woman. Though she was completely at home in the wilderness, and more competent than any woman he'd ever known, it was obvious that she was a total innocent in matters of men and women.

Which made her all the more interesting.

He tossed aside the blanket and sat up, gritting his teeth at the pain.

Outside the shelter, the countryside had been washed clean by the torrential rains. The thirsty soil had swallowed it up, leaving the land green and fresh.

Bo caught the fragrance of coffee and saw the blackened pot on the coals. With an effort he got to his feet and managed to cross the distance.

He was drinking his second cup of muddy coffee when Kitty came riding up. He felt his heart do a slow dance in his chest at the sight of her. Golden hair glinted in the sunlight, spilling down her back in a riot of tangles. Her slender female form was clearly outlined in the buckskin leggings and shirt.

"Good. You're up. You must be feeling stronger." She slid from the saddle, avoiding his eyes.

She'd told herself she wouldn't think about that little scene last night. But the minute she saw him, she felt herself blushing. "Think you're strong enough to sit a horse?"

He shrugged. "I guess that depends on how long I'll be riding."

"The better part of the day, I'd say. Misery is on the far side of those mountains."

He mentally groaned. Aloud he merely said, "Fine. When would you like to get started?"

"Now." She turned away, hoping he wouldn't see the relief on her face. Aaron had been alone far too long. At least that was the reason she was willing to admit to. In truth, she didn't want to spend another night alone out here in the wilderness with Bo Chandler. "I'll break camp while you eat some meat."

"I'm not hungry. I'll get myself dressed."

She gave a negligent shrug of her shoulders. "Suit yourself. I just figured you ought to eat something. You'll be needing your strength."

He knew she was right. Reluctantly he sliced off several pieces of meat and chewed on them while he pulled on his shirt and jacket, and jammed his feet into his boots. By the time he was strapping on his gun belt, Kitty had broken camp and was sitting astride her mare.

"Think you can pull yourself up behind me, or would you like some help?"

He heard the challenge in her tone and had to fight to keep his own casual. "I think I can manage."

He jammed a wide-brimmed hat on his head and climbed up behind her, wrapping his arms around her waist.

Feeling her flinch, he suddenly smiled. At least, if he had to endure discomfort, he wouldn't be the only one.

"Well, isn't this cozy?" He brought his mouth close to her ear and saw the way she shivered as he whispered, "I'm ready whenever you are, Kitty."

She dug her heels into the mare and they took off at a run.

Bo held on, feeling his body throb with every jarring motion.

It was one of those rare spring days in the Dakota Territory. The heat of the sun was tempered by the brisk wind blowing down from the Black Hills. Herds of buffalo grazed in the distance. The cottonwoods sported tender new leaves of pale green. Meadows were dotted with wild prairie roses and purple blooms of the Pasqueflower.

Bo nodded toward the herd. "Ever hunt buffalo?"

"A time or two." Kitty welcomed anything that would take her mind off the body pressed so close to hers. She was achingly aware of everything about him. The way his hands had lowered just enough to rest loosely at her hips. The way his thighs rubbed against the backs of hers. The way every word he spoke sent ripples of pleasure tingling along her spine.

"Every now and then Aaron gets a hankering for buffalo meat." She'd passed many miles telling Bo about the old man who had made a home for her and her brothers after they'd crossed the Badlands alone in search of their father. "Don't care much for buffalo meat myself. But at least once a year I try to get it for him as a special treat."

"It would take a whole lot of firepower to bring down one of those animals."

Kitty nodded. "Aaron has a buffalo rifle. A Sharps, breech-loading. First time I used it, it recoiled and knocked me out cold." She laughed at the memory. "When I woke up I was so mad, I fired again. And even though I forgot to aim, I managed to bag my first buffalo by accident."

That had Bo laughing along with her. "I'll bet you had quite a few bruises."

"I'll say. I had a black eye, a swollen cheek, and my shoulder was so tender I couldn't touch it for a week. Aaron thought I'd dislocated it, because it was so black and blue and purple and green." She laughed again. "I learned to have a whole lot of respect for buffalo rifles."

"That's a hard way to learn your lesson."

"That's how I've learned most everything." Her tone lowered with affection. "Aaron wasn't much for rules. Except for swearing. He said as long as my brothers and I lived under his roof, he'd tolerate no swearing."

Bo now understood her colorful language. She'd cleverly devised a more acceptable method of letting off steam.

"Aaron figured it was best if I found out for myself the right and wrong of things. But I knew he'd always be there if things didn't work out the way I'd wanted them to."

"He sounds like a good man."

"He's the best." She smiled, remembering the first time she'd seen him. "He sure doesn't look like much. He's missing a few teeth. He has to let his belt out a few notches every year. He calls himself a broken-down old rancher. But I don't care how he looks. He's really a guardian angel."

"Have you told him that?"

She shook her head. "I'd embarrass him. And myself. It's not something I could ever say to him. You'll see what I mean when you meet him."

"I'm looking forward to it." And he was, he realized. Especially after so many hours in the saddle.

If it hadn't been for the pleasure of Kitty's company, he'd have given up ten miles back and insisted
on time to rest his weary body. As it was, he knew
he was going on pure will. All that was keeping him
going now was the thought of sleeping in a real bed
tonight. In a real house. With real food.

Food.

He grinned, hoping Aaron would do the cooking
instead of Kitty.

It was nearly dusk when they came up over a
ridge and Kitty pointed. "There's our place."

Bo had a quick impression of a stingy herd of
cattle, a run-down shack and barn, and several corrals and sheds. Before he could take it all in, Kitty
put her fingers to her lips and let out an ear-splitting
whistle that would have carried for miles.

All Bo had time to do was hold on as Kitty's horse
took off at a full run. As they approached, a door
slammed and a slightly stooped, white-haired man
stepped out onto the porch, leaning on a tree limb
that had been whittled into a cane.

"Well." Aaron's face broke into a wide smile.
"You're home. About time."

Kitty brought her mount right to the edge of the

porch before swinging down from the saddle. "Did you miss me?"

"I always miss you, girl." Blackbird eyes glanced at the stranger. "You brought a visitor?"

She waited while Bo climbed stiffly from the back of the horse. "Aaron, meet Bo Chandler. Bo, this is Aaron Smiler."

The two men shook hands, each taking the measure of the other.

Up close, the old man's face was weathered and creased like aged leather. But the eyes looking into Bo's were as bright and inquisitive as a child's.

Kitty caught up the reins and started toward the corral. Over her shoulder she said, "Bo's mending from a gunshot. I told him he could stay with us awhile."

"A gunshot." Aaron continued studying the man. "Who shot you?"

"Three cowboys."

"Why'd they shoot you?"

"Near as I could figure, they wanted my horse."

"Why didn't you stop them?"

"I was distracted by the sight of a herd of mustangs. It was my first glimpse of wild horses, and I have to admit I was impressed. My attackers used that distraction to their advantage. I never even saw them coming."

It wasn't just the fancy words Bo used, but the

ease with which they seemed to roll off his tongue that had Aaron studying him a bit more closely. "You don't sound much like a cowboy. What are you doing in this part of the country?"

"I've never been to the Dakota Territory before. Figured it was time I saw just what everybody's talking about."

"Why would anybody be talking about the Dakotas?"

"Haven't you heard? There's talk in Washington that this territory might be considered for statehood."

Aaron shrugged. "What's that to us? Can Washington save our crops when the rains come too early? You think Washington will feed us if our herds die from predators or disease?"

Bo shook his head. "No, sir. But I believe there's strength in numbers. If the Dakotas join the rest of the United States, they qualify for federal marshals and soldiers and judges."

Aaron shot him a questioning look. "Which of those would you be?"

Bo grinned. "None of them. I'm just a citizen who wants to see this land, and experience it, from one shore to the other."

He watched as Kitty forked hay into the corral and filled a trough with water, before closing the gate and starting toward them.

Aaron stood to one side, his eyes narrowed in thought. "And what do you think about the Dakotas so far?"

"Prettiest sight I've ever seen." The minute the words were out of his mouth, he realized the old man was watching him carefully. Too carefully. And knew exactly what he'd meant.

Kitty climbed the steps to the porch. "What's for supper?"

Aaron tore his gaze from the stranger. "Whatever you can throw together, girl."

Bo nearly groaned in frustration. It looked like another night of barely edible food. He just hoped, since he had to suffer through another of Kitty's meals, that at least the bed would be soft.

Bo wasn't about to get his wish.

He lay on a blanket in front of the fireplace. From the next room came the sounds of Aaron's snores. In the loft above, Kitty had been asleep for an hour or more.

Dinner had been no better than what he'd eaten on the trail. The last of the venison had been sliced and fried until it was the consistency of an old boot. Kitty's biscuits were as hard as stones, and just about as tasteful. The milk had been warm and slightly curdled, and the coffee so hot he'd burned his tongue.

Neither Kitty nor Aaron had seemed to notice. They ate mechanically while Kitty brought the old man up to date on all that had transpired since she'd left. Then it had been Aaron's turn to tell her all his news, which seemed to consist mainly of growing debt.

"Jeb Simmons stopped by to pick up the mustang you owe him." Aaron turned to Bo and politely explained, "Jeb is a hog farmer a few hours north of here. Kitty usually barters a couple of hams for a horse or two." He turned back to Kitty. "When Jeb found out you weren't back yet, he said there'd be no more hams until you pay him what you already owe him."

"We don't need another ham." She drained her coffee. "We'll make do with beef and venison for the summer. It could be a month or more before I'll find another herd like the one that got away."

"What're we going to use to barter at Swensen's?"

Kitty glanced at Bo. "Olaf and Inga Swensen own the dry goods store in Misery. We get all our supplies there." She turned to Aaron. "Have the hens been laying?"

He nodded.

"All right then. Maybe Inga will take some eggs in trade for flour and sugar."

"And coffee," the old man said. "Don't forget the coffee."

She smiled. "How could I forget that? I've seen you the few times you've had to do without your coffee. I'd rather face a wounded she-bear protecting a cub."

Aaron merely chuckled before pouring himself another cup, and topping off Bo's cup, as well. He sat down and glanced at the young man, who hadn't said a word through the entire meal. "Now that you've had some food, you're probably more than ready to take yourself off to sleep."

"Yes, sir. But I'd like to help clean up the supper dishes first."

"Nonsense. You can barely keep your eyes open. Since Kitty did the cooking, I'll handle the cleaning up." Aaron nodded toward the closed door. "I'd invite you to share my big bed in the other room, but with my bum leg, I spend half the night tossing and turning. You'd never get any sleep in there."

Bo glanced at the loft. Seeing the direction of his gaze Aaron shook his head. "That's Kitty's bedroom, what there is of it. Even if it weren't, I'm betting you wouldn't even make it halfway up before you'd be asleep on your feet." He got up and left the room, returning minutes later with a bedroll. "You curl up on that rug in front of the fire, son. It may be a bit hard, but it'll be warm."

''Thanks. If you're sure you don't want my help in here…''

When Aaron gave a firm shake of his head, Bo shoved away from the table and crossed the room. After kicking off his boots, and crawling between the covers, he'd been asleep instantly.

Now, with the cabin still and dark as midnight, he found himself wide-awake and thinking over all he'd seen and heard.

It was apparent that Aaron and Kitty were barely able to make ends meet. Yet they seemed perfectly content here in this little shack in the middle of nowhere.

He'd been hoping to thank them for all their kindness and take his leave in the morning. Now he was wondering if he ought to reconsider. The place was practically falling down around them, and neither of them looked like they knew how to make even minor repairs.

Maybe he'd just stick around for a few days and lend a hand. It was the least he could do after what Kitty had done for him.

Kitty.

He smiled in the darkness. Time for a little honesty. He wasn't just sticking around merely to pay back a debt. He wanted a little more time with her. Time to look at her. Time to bask in the glow of the love she felt for the old man she thought of as a grandfather.

They were a fascinating pair. There was just something about the two of them that tugged at his heart.

What would it hurt to stay a few more days?

Pleased at his decision, he slept.

Chapter Four

"Looks like you're feeling some better this morning, son." Aaron limped out of the bedroom to find Bo sitting on the porch, drinking coffee. He sniffed the air. "Do I smell biscuits? Don't tell me Kitty's baking this early in the morning."

"Kitty's still asleep." Bo drained his cup and got to his feet. "I took the liberty of making biscuits and coffee. I hope you don't mind."

"Mind?" The old man looked astonished. "You mean you know how to cook?"

"Some." Bo moved past him and filled a cup with steaming coffee, then set several biscuits on a plate before handing it to him.

Aaron carried them out the door and settled himself in a chair. He spoke not a word as he devoured the biscuits and emptied the entire cup of coffee in one swallow. After several moments of silence, he gave a long, deep sigh. ''My Agnes used to bake biscuits like these. I haven't tasted the likes of them in many a year. Figured I'd probably have to wait until I joined her in the Promised Land to enjoy them again.''

Bo grinned. ''I'm glad they meet with your approval. Would you like more?''

''I shouldn't, but...'' The old man nodded and handed over his empty cup.

Minutes later Bo stepped onto the porch and handed Aaron a fresh cup of coffee and two more biscuits. Both men looked up when Kitty paused in the doorway.

At the sight of her, Bo's heart gave a hard quick tug. Her hair, a wild tangle of golden curls falling to her waist, looked like it had never seen a brush. The buckskin pants and shirt, which would have looked ridiculous on any other female, seemed so right for her. Her feet were bare. She was holding a pair of scuffed boots in one hand. In the other was a half-eaten biscuit.

She fixed Bo with a steely look. ''You make this?''

He nodded.

''I knew it couldn't have been Aaron. Why didn't you tell me you could cook?''

He shrugged. ''You never asked.''

She dropped the boots with a thud and turned

away. When she returned, she was eating another biscuit, which she washed down with coffee.

When she finished she sat down on a step and unselfconsciously began pulling on her boots. Over her shoulder she called, "You figuring on leaving today?"

"If it's all right with you and Aaron, I thought I'd stick around for a day or two."

Her hands stilled their movements. She'd been mentally preparing herself to say goodbye. She didn't know why her heart felt suddenly lighter. It certainly had nothing to do with Bo Chandler's decision to stay.

Instead of the smile that was in her heart, she frowned as she turned and forced herself to meet his eyes. "Why?"

"For one thing, that ride yesterday nearly did me in." Bo chuckled. "I think I need some time to heal my backside and regain my strength."

Hearing Aaron's snort of laughter he added, "And then there's these dressings." He touched a hand to the bulge at his shoulder. "I don't think I can change them myself. I might need a hand with them. That is, if you don't mind the extra work."

She glanced at Aaron, hoping he might volunteer his services. When he merely held his silence and stared into his cup, she tugged on her boot and got to her feet. "I'll deal with it later. Right now I've got work to see to."

She strolled off toward the corral and let herself inside. Minutes later she was astride her horse and heading toward the herd of cattle in the distance.

"Guess I'd better see to my own chores."

As Aaron took up his cane, Bo put a hand on his arm. "Why don't you sit in the sun awhile? I'll tend to whatever needs doing."

Without a word of protest the old man settled back in his chair. A short while later Bo handed him another cup of coffee before disappearing inside the house.

Aaron sipped his coffee, and lifted his face to the spring sunshine.

Something strange was going on here, though it was too soon to know exactly what. Kitty was acting like a mustang with a burr under her saddle. He'd never known her to be this nervous and jumpy. And this stranger, who had apparently lived a life of ease and spoke like a man with book learning, seemed perfectly content to sleep on the floor of a shack, doing mundane chores that most men would resist at any cost.

Not that he objected, Aaron thought with a sudden grin. Not as long as Bo Chandler agreed to make coffee that tasted like heaven and bake more of those biscuits that melted in the mouth.

He lifted his sore leg to the porch railing and leaned his head back. At his age he knew better than to try to figure out all the twists and turns along life's trail. He was just happy to go along for the ride, and see where it took him.

Kitty milked the cow, then worked up a sweat mucking the stalls. It was filthy, backbreaking work, especially since nothing had been done in the barn while she'd been gone.

She couldn't fault Aaron. There was simply too much work for one tired old man. If she could just get a little money set aside, she'd hire on some help. Jesse Cutler, who ran the barbershop and bath in Misery, had a houseful of boys. Any one of them would be willing to help with the chores around here, if she could just afford to pay them.

She sighed, and forked dung into a wagon. That herd of mustangs would have gone a long way toward easing their burden. As soon as she caught up her chores around here, she'd have to backtrack and see if she could find any trace of them. Of course, it would mean leaving Aaron alone again. Was it her imagination, or did he seem to be moving a bit slower than before? Each time she was forced to leave him for any length of time, she had the feeling when she returned that she could see a change in him. And regrettably, not a change for the better.

She felt a quick hitch around her heart and brushed the thought aside. She couldn't even begin to imagine life without Aaron. He was her rock. Her lifeline. Hers, she thought with a greedy fervor that had her setting her teeth as she lifted yet another load of dung to the wagon. Though they'd met as strangers, he had become her grandfather. His was the only home she could remember. That other place of her childhood had been consigned to a small, dark corner of her mind.

To keep from thinking about the future, she began working ever harder, until the stalls were spread with fresh hay, and the wagonload of dung had been hauled to the fields and worked into the soil.

Bone-weary and caked with mud and dung, Kitty made her way to the cabin and climbed the steps to the porch.

The first thing she noticed was a pail of fresh water beside the door, along with some soap and a clean linen towel. She rolled the sleeves of her buckskin shirt and sank her arms gratefully into the water, soaping and rinsing, before splashing water over her face.

It felt so wonderful, she couldn't resist plunging her head in, as well. She ducked below the water, soaping her scalp. After several more times under water she came up sputtering, and shook her head like a puppy, sending a shower of water over everything nearby. She took no notice of the way her clothes were soaked as she wrapped her hair and gave it a vigorous toweling before sitting on the steps and kicking off her boots.

She was still sitting there, wiggling her toes and feeling gloriously cool and fresh, when the door opened. Aaron poked his head out and gave the ear-splitting whistle that had become their signal to each other.

When he caught sight of her he gave a sheepish grin. "Sorry. Thought you were still out in the field. Supper's ready."

She got to her feet and followed him inside, where she lifted her head and breathed in the most amazing aromas. "What do I smell?"

"Bo baked bread."

"Bread." Her mouth was already watering.

"And he's had beef roasting on the fire for hours. If it tastes half as good as it smells, I'd say we're going to be mighty satisfied tonight."

Just then Bo stepped through the doorway behind her.

Kitty glanced at the butter churn in his hands, which had been gathering dust for years in the barn. "What're you doing with that?"

"I believe it's used to churn butter. Though not lately, I assume. I figured I'd put some of that warm milk to good use." He stared admiringly at the way the wet buckskin leggings hugged every line and curve of her thighs and bottom. "I see you took advantage of the soap and water."

"Yes. Thanks."

"You're welcome." He pointed toward the table, already set for a meal. "Why don't you and Aaron sit. Everything's ready. I'm sure after the day you've put in, you must be starving."

"I figure right about now I could eat half a cow. Raw," she added.

When she and Aaron were seated, Bo set down a loaf of perfectly browned bread, with steam still rising from it. Kitty lifted a sharp knife and started to saw through it. Her eyes widened when the knife cut through it like butter.

Bo loaded a platter with beef so tender it fell off the bone where it lay swimming in gravy. Kitty helped herself to some, then in turn held the platter for Aaron, before handing it back to Bo.

They ate in silence for several minutes before Kitty gave a sigh of pure pleasure. "This is wonderful."

Bo grinned. "I'm glad you like it."

"Like it? I don't believe I've ever tasted anything as fine as this." She shot him a suspicious look. "Where'd you learn to cook like this?"

He shrugged. "All the men in my family liked to

cook. My father used to say it relaxed him. I feel the same way.''

Aaron swallowed a mouthful of beef before asking, ''Your folks still alive, Bo?''

''No, sir. My mother was the first to go. I watched my father nurse her through a long illness that had her bedridden. After that, he seemed to lose heart. I always thought my father just didn't want to go on without the woman he'd called his lifelong sweetheart.''

Kitty felt a shiver along her spine. She'd never heard anyone talk so openly and lovingly about family before.

She slathered butter on a slice of warm bread and ate it slowly, savoring every bite. ''Bo's family raised horses in Virginia.''

Aaron smiled. ''I've heard Virginia's fine horse country.''

Bo nodded. ''Actually, my grandfather was the horseman. My father was more a gentleman farmer. But his real love was the law.''

Aaron lifted a brow. ''You don't say? Was he a lawyer or a judge?''

''Both. He had a law practice in Virginia before the war. Afterward, he divided his time between Virginia and Washington.'' He held out the platter. ''More beef?''

Aaron shook his head, resisting a third helping,

and sat back, sipping coffee. "What did your father do in Washington?"

"He was put in charge of finding ways to heal the country."

Aaron studied him over the rim of his cup. "Not an easy job, I'd say."

"No sir. I watched him agonize over all the injustices he found in both the North and the South. He said there would always be men trying to take advantage of other men while they were down. He saw the law as the only way to redress the wrongs being committed."

"You must have been proud of the work your pa did."

Bo nodded. "I was. That's why I decided to study law."

"You're a lawyer?"

"Yes, sir."

Aaron heard the note of pride in the young man's voice as he set down his cup. "This was a fine meal, Bo. I thank you."

"You're welcome. It's the least I can do to thank you for your hospitality."

Kitty seemed distracted as she tried to jiggle the arm of her chair.

Aaron looked over. "What's wrong?"

"I don't know." She tried again. "Did you fix this while I was chasing those mustangs?"

"I didn't even know it needed fixing."

Bo stood and retrieved the coffeepot, filling their cups as he rounded the table. He paused beside her chair. "I fixed it today when I noticed that it was about to fall off."

While he returned the coffeepot to the stove, Kitty and Aaron exchanged matching looks of surprise.

"Well." Aaron gave a wide smile. "It seems you can do just about everything."

Bo shrugged. "I enjoy tinkering. But there's one thing I can't do." He touched a hand to the dressings that ran from his chest to his back. "I tried changing these today, but I just couldn't stretch my arms far enough."

"Mending critters is Kitty's specialty." Aaron shoved back his chair. "I've been saving a couple of cigars for a special occasion, Bo. Why don't you join me out on the porch?"

"I'd like that."

Aaron turned to Kitty. "Do we have any more of that whiskey in the cupboard?"

She nodded and went to fetch it. "I think there's enough for a couple of tumblers."

Aaron paused at the door. "You might want to save a little to pour on Bo's wound."

He saw her frown before she turned away.

Minutes later they sat in the gathering shadows, Aaron in his chair, Bo on the steps, smoke curling over their heads, glasses of whiskey in their hands. Kitty sipped the last of the coffee and leaned her back against the porch rail, looking up at the sky, awash with millions of stars.

Her voice sounded dreamy. "Of all the places you've been, Bo, which one did you like best?"

He drew on his cigar and expelled a wreath of smoke. "It'd be hard to choose just one. In Boston and New York you can feel the sense of power from old money and education. In San Francisco there's a sense of adventure, and the money is mostly new. But when I leave the big cities and get back to the land, that's where I feel connected to real people. Folks just want to be left alone to work the fields, raise the herds, and have a sense of their own destiny."

"Is that what you're looking for, son?"

Bo glanced at Aaron. "I think so. I don't know why I felt so compelled to leave home. I guess I just figured my heart would tell me when I'd found whatever it was I was searching for."

Kitty drained her cup and set it aside. "I can't imagine any reason strong enough to take me away from here."

Aaron stubbed out his cigar and got slowly to his feet. "Neither can I." He gave them both a smile. "I'll say good-night now."

Kitty stood up, eager to escape. ''I'll go with you, Aaron.''

''You're forgetting Bo's dressing. Better see to it, so there's no infection, girl.'' He turned away and let himself into the cabin, leaving Kitty alone on the porch with Bo.

Chapter Five

"**W**ell. We'd best get to it." Determined to get this over with, Kitty held up the bottle of whiskey and studied it by the light of the moon. "Good thing Aaron cautioned me to save a little of this. There's just enough left to pour on that wound."

She removed the cork and turned to find Bo just easing his shirt from his shoulders. The sight of the muscles across his back sent an odd little feeling deep inside her. When he turned toward her, she could see him smiling.

"Seems like I've been undressing for you ever since we first met." He began unwinding the dressing, easing it away from his torn flesh. Then he stood waiting for Kitty to make the next move.

She stepped closer and made a motion with her hand. "Turn around."

He did as she asked and she gingerly removed the

rest of the dressing, exposing the wound. As she did, her fingers brushed his skin and she pulled her hand back quickly. To cover the ripple of feelings, she dumped a generous amount of whiskey on the puckered flesh.

He sucked in a breath, then slowly let it out as he turned. Seeing her hesitate, he took the bottle from her hands and poured the remaining whiskey on his chest before handing her the empty bottle.

"Sorry." Kitty swallowed. In the silence, the sound seemed overly loud in her ears. "But I didn't want to hurt you again." A lie, she knew. She hadn't wanted to risk touching him again. The shock had been a jolt to her system. In fact, everything about Bo Chandler was a shock to her system.

"That's all right." His voice, low and deep, sent shivers along her spine. "My father used to say that sometimes there has to be hurting before there can be healing." He handed her some clean linen strips. "If you'd tie these I'd be obliged."

"You're too tall." She glanced toward Aaron's chair. "You'd better sit there."

He sat and tilted his head upward, watching her while she wound the linen strips around his chest to his back several times. The feel of her hands on his naked flesh was the sweetest of tortures. It occurred to him that if Kitty knew what she was doing to him, she'd either run inside her cabin and lock the door against him, or pull her gun and shoot him dead where he sat.

"Aaron was right. You're good at this, Kitty. How did you learn?"

"Necessity." She gave a nervous laugh. "My brothers were always getting bloodied over something."

"Tell me about your brothers." He figured that might put them both at ease.

Kitty was grateful for something to talk about. "Gabe's the oldest. He's the sheriff in Misery. Yale's two years younger than Gabe. He used to be a gambler, until he took himself a wife and settled down on a ranch outside of town." She was babbling, she knew. But it kept her from thinking about the way she felt each time she touched him. "With all their scrapping and gunfights, I found out early that I don't get skittish at the sight of blood."

Of course, tending to her brothers wasn't at all the same as tending to this man. She tied the ends of the dressing carefully, then stepped back.

Bo got to his feet, towering over her. "What does make you skittish, Kitty?"

You, she thought. This.

She tossed her head. "There's not much I'm afraid of."

"Is that so?" He touched a hand to her hair. Just a touch, but he saw her smile fade and her eyes go wide. "Is it just me, Kitty? Or do you react to all men this way?"

"What way?"

"You have the same look in your eyes those mustangs had when they heard that gunshot. Like you're about to make a run for it."

"What I'm feeling isn't fear. It's anger." She slapped his hand away and started to turn.

"Is that why you're running?"

"I'm not…"

It happened so quickly, she had no time to react. His hand closed over her shoulder, holding her when she tried to walk away. In one smooth motion he turned her into his arms. The look in his eyes had her heart leaping to her throat. She had no doubt that he intended to kiss her.

"Don't you dare…"

The words died on her lips as his mouth covered her in a kiss so hot, so hungry, it stole the very breath from her lungs. In her entire life, she'd never been kissed. There had been a few cowboys who'd tried, but they'd quickly backed off when they saw the way Kitty Conover reacted to their clumsy attempts at lovemaking. Before their eyes this little female could turn herself into a fiery executioner armed with both pistol and knife. There wasn't a single cowboy in the Dakota Territory who had ever tried to kiss her a second time.

''Shh. It's too late.'' He whispered the words inside her mouth as he took the kiss deeper.

He hadn't planned this. In fact, all he'd wanted was to tease her about being afraid of him. But now that he was holding her, kissing her, he couldn't seem to stop. Her lips were so incredibly soft. Her mouth so perfectly formed. He could feel himself sinking into her. The need, sharp and swift, had the blood pounding in his temples.

As he lingered over her lips he could taste the fear on them. And something more. The first faint stirrings of passion.

She tasted as fresh, as clean as a clear mountain stream. There was no artifice in her. No hint of sultry seduction. There was only innocence. And surprise. That made it all the sweeter. And the need all the more compelling.

He wasn't even aware that he'd backed her up until she was pressed firmly against the porch railing. And still he continued kissing her while his hands moved along her back, igniting fires up and down her spine.

Kitty knew she ought to resist. But she couldn't find the will. Instead she seemed lost in the wonder of these strange new feelings. How could a man's mouth be this clever? How could his hands hold her so gently, so carefully, as though she were a fragile doll?

She knew she could walk away and he wouldn't keep her against her will. And yet she couldn't move. She felt anchored to the spot, as surely as one of her mustangs caught in a lasso.

His lips were so sure, so practiced, as they moved over hers with such skill. He tasted of whiskey, and faintly of tobacco. The warmth of his skin seemed to pour into her, causing her own flesh to heat and her bones to melt. She was afraid if she stayed here much longer she would simply slide through his fingers and pour like water to the ground.

Somehow her arms had found their way around his waist. Except for the clean dressings, his skin was bare and warm to the touch. So warm it nearly burned her palms where they were pressed to his back. He changed the angle of the kiss and she felt the ripple of muscles under her hand. It was the most purely sensual thing she'd ever experienced.

"Bo." His name was a cry on her lips. A plea for help.

Hearing it, he lifted his head and struggled for some sense of sanity. How was it possible that in those few moments, he'd completely lost himself in the pure pleasure of her kiss?

With his hands at her shoulders he held her a little away and stared down into her eyes. She looked as dazed as he felt.

"You'd…better get inside now, Kitty."

She tried to speak, but no words came out. Instead she merely nodded her head and took a step to one side, hoping she wouldn't stumble. At the door to the cabin she turned back to see him standing perfectly still, watching her. There was something dark and brooding in his eyes that frightened her, even while it excited her. Like a wild stallion, before mating.

Without a word she hurried inside and climbed the ladder to her loft.

It seemed a long time later that she heard Bo let himself into the cabin. From her position above she watched as he kicked off his boots and climbed between the covers. He lay with his hands behind his head, and she had the uneasy feeling that, even though he couldn't see her in the darkness, he was staring straight at her. It caused her heart to speed up and gave her an odd fluttering deep inside.

She snuggled into her nest of furs and closed her eyes. But the thought of Bo Chandler holding her, kissing her, stayed with her long into the night, robbing her of precious sleep.

''How's your wound this morning, son?'' Aaron walked out of his bedroom to the wonderful fragrance of coffee simmering over the fire, and thick slices of bread browning over the coals.

"It feels some better. The pain seems a little less sharp now when I move."

"That's good news. I told you Kitty has the healing touch."

"Yes, sir. You did." Bo filled a cup and handed it to the old man, then retrieved the toast, slathering it with fresh butter before setting it on a plate.

Aaron took a bite of toast. "You realize, of course, that you're spoiling me."

"That's my intention."

Aaron chuckled. "When you leave here, it'll be all the harder to bear my own cooking." He smiled. "Or Kitty's."

"I tasted Kitty's cooking on the trail."

That brought a snort of laughter from the old man. "It's a wonder you survived. But I have nobody to blame but myself. I taught her everything she knows."

"Then you can be proud. She may not be much of a cook or housekeeper, but she's one fine woman."

Something in the way he said it had Aaron studying him more closely.

Just then Kitty climbed down the ladder and dropped her boots by the fire before crossing to the table.

"'Morning," she said to no one in particular before ducking her head.

"Good morning. Coffee?" Bo held out a steaming cup and she was forced to take it from his hands. As she did, she felt the tingle in her fingers and looked away quickly.

Instead of sitting down at the table, she crossed to the fireplace and set down her cup while she pulled on her boots. "I've been thinking I might leave today and see if I can pick up the trail of that mustang herd I lost."

"Today?" Aaron frowned. "Girl, you've only just returned home. Can't it wait?"

She shrugged, avoiding his eyes. "We need the money. Besides, I figured Bo could keep you company. That is, if he's planning on staying a couple more days."

"I could stay." Bo studied the rigid line of her back.

"How long do you figure to be gone?" Aaron's coffee lay forgotten on the table.

"As long as it takes, I guess." She strapped on her gun belt, and picked up her rifle and cowhide duster.

When she turned and saw the look on Aaron's face, she crossed to him and laid a hand on his arm. Her tone softened. "We need this herd. They'll bring in enough money to pay all our bills. Don't worry. It shouldn't take me long. Now that I know the stallion's habits and his favorite places to graze, I figure I'll be back in no time.''

"You take care of yourself, girl."

She nodded. "I will."

She started toward the door, keeping her face averted. "'Bye, Bo. Take care of Aaron."

"Yeah." As she started toward the barn he wrapped a loaf of bread in a linen square and poured coffee into a canteen. Seeing Aaron watching him he gave the old man a smile. "Just a few provisions she can take with her."

He let himself out of the cabin and made his way to the barn, where Kitty was saddling her mare. When she caught sight of him she tightened the cinch and picked up the reins to lead her horse outside.

He stood in her way, forcing her to look at him for the first time.

"You're doing this because of what happened last night, aren't you?"

She lifted her chin. "What's that supposed to mean?"

"It means you're running away. You'd rather go back out on the trail than face up to what you felt last night."

"What I felt last night was…annoyance." She knew her face was flaming at the blatant lie. But he'd backed her into a corner. Now she had no choice but to fight with whatever weapon she could find. "As for running, I've never run from anything in my life. And I'm certainly not running from the likes of you, Bo Chandler."

"Aren't you?"

"No."

"Liar." He was surprised by the rush of anger. He'd always prided himself on his ability to keep his feelings on a tight rein. But there was something about this ornery female that seemed to bring out the worst in him. Without giving a thought to what he was doing he caught her roughly by the shoulders and dragged her close, covering her mouth with his.

The flare of passion caught them both by surprise.

With a muttered oath he took the kiss deeper, savaging her mouth.

She made a guttural sound that seemed more animal than human. Her hands dug into the back of his head, though she had no way of knowing how they got there.

He drove her back against the rough wood of the stall, his hands gripping her tightly, his mouth fused to hers in a kiss so hot, so hungry, it seemed to send off sparks.

This wasn't so much a kiss as a tug-of-war. There seemed a barely contained sense of urgency that had them both taking, giving, then taking more. But beneath the thin veil of anger was something much more intense. A sense of deep, primal passion.

When at last they lifted their heads, they stood, chests heaving, bodies trembling, taking great gulps of air into their starving lungs.

Bo pressed both hands against the stall behind her head, needing to steady himself. Kitty was grateful that he didn't move. She was afraid if he did she might sink to her knees in the hay.

When he could trust his voice he managed to say, "I believe I just proved my point."

"You proved nothing." She was surprised at how difficult it was to speak. Her heart was still racing like a herd of mustangs. "Except what an arrogant, pigheaded, flea-bitten piece of cow dung you are."

At any other time he might have laughed at her attempt at swearing. Right now his blood was still too hot, his passion barely under control.

"I didn't take you for a liar or a coward, Kitty. But right now you're lying, and running away to cover it up."

She pushed away from him and strode toward her horse. When she'd managed to pull herself into the saddle she stared down at him with a look of fury. "Men have died for those words."

"Then kill me if you're saying I'm wrong."

She ignored his challenge and urged her horse into a run.

Bo stood in the doorway and watched as horse and rider sped off across the field. Then he noticed the linen-wrapped parcels lying in the dirt.

It didn't matter, he told himself as he retrieved them and started toward the cabin. But he knew it did. It was just one more thing he'd worry about until she returned.

Damn her. He'd invited her to kill him. That's just what she was doing. One heartbeat at a time.

When he'd come to the Badlands, he hadn't expected to find anyone like Kitty Conover. Or to feel the out-of-control emotions he'd been feeling since meeting her.

He stalked back to the cabin, determined to put that damnable little female out of his mind.

Chapter Six

Kitty knelt in the tall grass and studied the herd of mustangs nearby. A stallion stood watch while more than a dozen mares grazed. This wasn't the herd she'd hoped to find, but they were too good to pass up. She'd only been out on the trail a few hours. If she could lasso the stallion, she could have the entire herd back in her corral before suppertime. Tomorrow she could start breaking them to saddle. By next week she would have enough money to buy spring supplies. Seed. Grain. She smiled. And maybe enough to buy a jar of honey.

Her brother Yale had always teased her about her sweet tooth. And whenever he'd return from one of his many journeys, his pockets bulging with gambling money, he would have a jar of honey for his little sister. Of course, that had all changed now that he'd settled down with his beloved Cara and become a respectable citizen in the town of Misery.

Not that he neglected her and Aaron. It was just that he was busy now with his new wife and family. As was her older brother, Gabe.

It was still hard for Kitty to imagine both Gabe and Yale with wives. The three Conovers had all been so wild and reckless and free. She'd truly believed they would always remain that way.

How could they have given up their freedom so willingly? Both her brothers seemed so happy now. So content with their new lives. Still, it didn't seem possible that one person could make such a difference in another person's life. How had they known if they were doing the right thing? Did they ever wake in the night and worry that it might all be some horrible mistake?

The stallion lifted his head and pawed the earth. The sudden movement jolted Kitty out of her reverie. She had to move quickly if she wanted to catch this herd before they decided to move on.

Crouching down, she returned to her horse and eased herself into the saddle, removing the lasso as she did. By the time her mare was moving ahead, she was already swinging the rope. When it encircled the stallion's neck, the animal reared and snorted, before trying to run. In anticipation, Kitty was already twisting the rope around the saddle horn while her horse pulled back slightly. Seconds later she was out of the saddle and tossing a second lasso over the stallion's head, tying the other end of the rope to a nearby tree.

The stallion fought the ropes, bucking, rearing, twisting. All the while the rest of his herd stood on a distant hill and watched in fear.

When he finally began to tire, Kitty eased her mare closer, allowing the rope to go slack. The stallion continued standing perfectly still, watching her.

"I know you don't like me." Kitty kept her voice low and soothing as she slid from the saddle and began to untie the rope attached to the tree. "But you'll have a good life...."

She felt pain crash through her as she was thrown to the ground. Looking up she saw the stallion rearing to attack again. Though she managed to roll aside, dodging the worst of the blow, she saw stars as his hooves made contact with her shoulder.

She had the presence of mind to crawl into the grass, just out of reach of those menacing hooves, as the stallion thrashed about beside her. Thankfully the rope still tied to her mare kept him from getting any closer.

For long minutes Kitty lay, struggling not to give in to the pain that was threatening to take her down. She couldn't afford to lose consciousness here, where no one would find her. But the pain was so severe, she could hardly catch her breath.

Her ribs were broken, she knew instinctively as

she touched a hand to the spot. At least a few of them. And probably her shoulder.

She had to get home. Somehow she had to find the strength to get back in the saddle and get herself safely home.

It was the last coherent thought she had before the darkness overtook her.

"Thought I heard some hammering." Aaron leaned on his cane as he walked to the door of the cabin, looking rumpled from his nap by the fire.

Bo was just easing his shoulder against the door as he secured the new hinge. "This looked like it was about to fall off."

"It's been that way for a year or more." Aaron gave an embarrassed laugh. "Been meaning to get to it. Things seem to have a way of getting away from me these days."

"It takes a heap of work to keep a place this size running." As he straightened, Bo rubbed at his tender wound.

"You're hurting, son." Aaron stepped through the doorway onto the porch. "It's too soon for you to be doing all this work."

Bo shook his head. "I don't mind. I've never liked being idle."

"Me, either." Aaron eased himself onto his chair on the porch. "Though you wouldn't know it to look

at me now, there was a time when I could do everything that needed doing around here. Now I move
like a snail and can barely get through each day.''

''No need to explain.'' Bo retrieved his tools.
''I'm impressed by all you and Kitty have managed
to do here.'' He sat on the top step and leaned his
back against the rail. ''Kitty told me how you took
her and her brothers in when they wandered here
from the Badlands.''

Aaron smiled remembering. ''They looked pretty
rough. Gabe, the oldest, trying to be both father and
mother. Yale, tough-talking and ready to take on the
world. And Kitty. She looked just like a little angel.
The prettiest face I'd ever seen, framed by all those
soft golden curls. At first I was afraid I'd have some
frail little doll on my hands. One who would sniffle
and cry at the least little thing. Instead, I found myself with a wildcat on my hands. I think she may be
the toughest of them all.''

Bo grinned. ''I've never met a female like her.
You taught her well.''

Aaron returned his smile. ''She's something, isn't
she? By the time she was nine or ten she could do
anything on the ranch that her brothers could do.
When it comes to horses, she's a natural. Of course,
it would have been nice if she'd taken to a few female things. Like cooking and cleaning. But she always got her back up when one of us would mention

it.'' He shook his head, remembering. ''She just wanted to be like Gabe and Yale. She resented even the suggestion that she couldn't do everything they could do.''

He glanced at the sun, just beginning to set over the rims of the Black Hills in the distance. ''She'll be making camp soon.''

Bo could hear the wistful note in the old man's voice. ''You miss her, don't you?''

Aaron seemed embarrassed. ''I surely do. I never thought, when I took in three scared little orphans, they'd take over my life so completely. I was already in my sunset years, with my own wife and sons dead and buried. And those three just filled a hole in my heart I didn't even know I had.''

''Then it's a lucky thing you found each other.''

Aaron gave him a gentle smile. ''Son, I don't believe in luck. What happened was meant to be. Just the way Kitty was meant to find you when you'd been shot in the middle of nowhere.''

Bo looked thoughtful as he got to his feet. ''I'd better check on our supper.''

Kitty opened her eyes and gave a low moan of pain. She could see, by the way the sun had made its arc across the sky, that she'd been unconscious for some time. Nearby the stallion gave a snort of impatience, and her mare gave an answering whinny.

Her mare. She had to get to her horse without being stomped to death by the stallion. She got to her knees and felt the world give a sickening spin. She waited until her head cleared, then began dragging herself toward her mare, giving the mustang a wide berth.

By the time she'd made it to her horse, she was bathed in sweat and her face was contorted in pain. Still, by pulling herself up to the stirrups, she managed to haul herself into the saddle.

The stallion tossed its head in defiance. Seeing it, Kitty gritted her teeth. "I'm not cutting you loose. Not after all you cost me." She urged her mare closer and leaned over to untie the rope from the tree. Then she coiled it, along with the other rope, around her saddle horn. "You may be able to break one rope. I don't think you're strong enough to break two."

She turned her mare toward home, with the stallion moving along on one side, and had the satisfaction of seeing the herd following at a distance.

Every movement caused excruciating pain that had her clenching her teeth to keep from crying out. Her buckskins, drenched in sweat, felt cold and clammy in the evening air.

When at last she came up over a ridge and saw Aaron's cabin in the distance, she knew she could go no farther. She pulled out her rifle and gave two quick shots in succession, the signal she and Aaron had always used in case of trouble. Then she slumped over the neck of her mare, praying she could hold on until help came.

"What's that?" Bo looked up from the table at the sound of gunshots.

Aaron was out of his chair and limping across the room, reaching for his rifle. It was the fastest Bo had ever seen him move.

"Kitty." The old man turned toward the door, leaning heavily on his cane. "That's the signal we've always used when one of us is in trouble."

Bo grabbed up his gun belt from a nail by the door and strapped it on as he dashed across the porch.

Behind him he could hear the thumping of Aaron's cane as the old man followed him out the door.

"Up there," Aaron shouted.

Bo was already running across the field, heading toward the shadowy figures on the hill in the distance. He could make out Kitty's horse in the lead, with several more slightly behind. At first he thought there was no one in the saddle. But as he drew nearer he could make out a figure that seemed to be clinging to the mare's mane.

"Kitty." He reached up and hauled her into his arms.

"Bo?" The word was little more than a whisper. "I didn't want to worry Aaron, but I..." Pain crashed through her and she sucked in a breath.

"Shh." He cradled her against his chest. "Don't talk, Kitty. Save your strength."

"The mustangs..."

He glanced at the stallion, tied firmly behind her mare, and the herd, standing back a hundred yards or more, watching nervously.

"They're here. I'll bring them in. But right now I'm getting you to the cabin."

"Bring...now." She gasped, then said through gritted teeth, "Don't want them...get away."

"You never let up, do you?" With a snarl of impatience he looped the reins around his arm, leading her horse as he began carrying her toward the cabin. And though every step must have caused her unbearable pain, she endured in silence.

Aaron was waiting near the corral.

"Is she...?"

"She's alive. But hurting. And she insisted I bring this mustang in."

The old man sighed. "That's my Kitty."

He opened the gate to the corral and Bo led the mare and stallion inside. The old man fumbled with the ropes, releasing them from the saddle horn, be-

fore leading the mare out of the corral, and leaving
the stallion alone inside.

Bo motioned toward the herd in the distance.
''What about them?''

''This fellow's their leader. As long as he's locked
up here, they won't go far. We'll worry about round-
ing them up tomorrow.'' Aaron turned toward the
cabin. ''Let's get Kitty inside and take a look at her
wounds.''

As Bo carried her up the steps and into the cabin,
he looked down at the woman in his arms, lying as
still as death. He would never be able to forget the
sheer terror he'd experienced when he'd first caught
sight of her slumped in that saddle.

Even now, knowing she was alive, he wasn't sure
his poor heart would ever be the same again.

Chapter Seven

Bo knelt on the rug before the fire and laid Kitty down as gently as he could manage. Still, that simple movement had her sucking in a breath.

"Sorry." His touch was soft as he began to probe for injuries. "It appears your arm's broken. Maybe the shoulder, too. Where else are you hurting?"

"Ribs." She touched a hand to the spot and found his fingers already there, probing gently.

He nodded to Aaron. "We'll need some clean linen to bind her. That ought to ease the pain a little. Then we'll have to set that arm."

The old man hobbled away and returned with a bar of lye soap, a flask, and several linen towels that he began tearing into strips.

Bo opened the flask and almost gagged at the fumes. "What's this?"

"Elixir. At least that's what the traveling salesman called it. I figure it's some wood alcohol. Mountain whiskey. I keep it for emergencies.'' He grinned. "It may be old and smell worse than a sow's breath, but it ought to do the trick.''

"If it doesn't kill her first.''

Bo watched as Aaron gently lifted Kitty's head and held the flask to her lips. "Take a couple of healthy swallows of this, girl.''

She wrinkled her nose, but he gave her no chance to resist as he pressed it to her mouth and poured it down her throat. Though she choked and grumbled, he managed to force down several swallows before she resolutely clamped her mouth shut, refusing any more.

Aaron corked the flask and turned away, tearing more linen strips. "Give that a few minutes to take effect, and she won't care what you do to her.''

"You sure of that?'' Bo eyed the old man suspiciously.

Aaron merely shrugged. "You'll see for yourself soon enough.''

"We'll need to get at her arm.'' Bo took the knife from Kitty's waist and offered it to the old man. "You'll have to get that shirt off her.''

Aaron shook his head firmly. "I handled the whiskey. Now it's your turn. I wouldn't advise you to try it until the elixir has a chance to do its work.''

Bo watched Kitty's eyes trying to focus on him

as he began cutting away the sleeve of her blood-stained buckskin shirt. When she became aware of what he was doing, she gave a halfhearted slap at his hand.

"Don't think…taking advantage of me," she muttered. "Just because you're good-looking."

"Really? You think so?" He couldn't help grinning.

She made a purring sound. "Even better-looking than Jack Slade."

"Who's that?" Bo turned to Aaron.

"Jack owns the Red Dog Saloon in Misery. Quite the ladies' man. When he's not taking the local cowboys in a game of poker."

Kitty lifted a hand to Bo's cheek. "You're prettier'n Slade." She turned to Aaron. "Much prettier. Don't you think?" Her arm dropped heavily to her side.

Bo was still grinning. "We've got to set that arm, Kitty."

"Set it?" She touched a hand to the spot, but couldn't seem to feel it. "On the shelf? All right." She gave a dreamy smile. "If you say so."

Aaron chuckled. "See? That old elixir does it every time." He nodded toward the knife in Bo's hand. "You can go ahead now, son. She's off in her own world."

Bo cut the shirt, exposing enough flesh to do a

proper job, but managing to leave enough of her torso covered to satisfy the dignity of the old man who was kneeling beside him.

As he began washing the area with lye soap, both men gasped when they realized the extent of her wound.

"This was no fall from a horse," Bo said between clenched teeth.

"I'd say she had a taste of that stallion's temper."

Bo swiveled his head. "You mean he attacked her?"

Aaron nodded. "Wouldn't be the first time. Not that she's careless. But when you deal with wild critters, you have to be ready to endure some pain."

"Some?" Bo probed the wound, then looked up suddenly. "This shoulder is separated."

"You sure about that, son?"

Bo looked grim. "I can feel it. And right now, while she's in that other world, we're going to have to get it back into place."

The old man took the leather sheath that hung at Kitty's waist and put it between her teeth, before taking hold of her by the other arm. "Do what you have to. Then we'll deal with these broken bones."

"Hold her steady." Bo took hold of her shoulder and gave a sudden wrenching pull. The sound of her shoulder snapping into place was drowned by the scream that echoed up from her throat and came out in a long piercing cry.

As they laid her gently back down on the rug, they could see that she'd slipped into a place where there was no more pain. Only blessed darkness.

Aaron shuffled toward his bedroom, and bumped into the wall before making it through the doorway. After hearing Kitty's scream, and watching Bo set her arm and bind her ribs, he'd helped himself to a bit of the foul-smelling elixir to ease the pain in his heart. Now he knew he had to give up and sleep, or he'd embarrass himself by passing out right here.

He turned and pointed with his cane. "You might as well sleep in Kitty's bed up in the loft. She won't be needing it."

Bo shook his head. "I'll be fine here. She might wake through the night. If she does, she's going to be in a lot of pain."

"You'll give her the elixir?"

Bo nodded. "Don't worry, Aaron. I'll see to it."

"Good night then." The old man turned and nearly toppled over before closing his door.

Bo pulled a chair close to the fire and settled himself in it. Earlier he'd climbed to Kitty's sleeping loft and retrieved some fur throws. Now she slept, wrapped in a warm cocoon. But every once in a while she whimpered in her sleep, and he knew it was only a matter of time before the pain would wake her.

He sat studying her with a sense of amazement at what she'd endured. The pain from the stallion's hooves must have been excruciating, but she'd managed to make her way home.

Home.

He glanced around at the simple little shack. On his father's farm in Virginia, this would have been considered little more than a storage shed. But to Kitty and her brothers it must have seemed a palace after surviving a trek across the Badlands. Besides, it wasn't the condition of the building that mattered, but rather the love and security they'd come to find here with Aaron Smiler.

He was an extraordinary old man, who'd taken on three more mouths to feed when he'd barely had enough to feed himself. Bo thought of the lessons he'd learned at his father's knee. Honesty. Integrity. Service to his fellow man. Aaron had no time to preach about them. He'd lived those lessons every day of his life.

Bo glanced again at Kitty and felt an odd stirring at the sight of her hair, matted and dirty, spilling around that angel face. There was something about her that tugged at his heart. From the first moment he'd seen her, he'd been intrigued. She was unlike any female he'd ever known before. Wild. Free. And hell-bent on being in charge of her own life.

He admired that more than he cared to admit. Wasn't that what he'd been seeking for himself when he'd set out on this odyssey? He'd had this powerful need to travel the length of this country from shore to shore. To see the people who had been affected by the terrible war that had wrenched a nation apart. He'd left all that was comfortable and familiar, to explore all that was foreign to him. In doing so, he hoped to find a place that would call out to him. A place where he would truly feel at home.

Weary beyond belief, he stretched his long legs out toward the warmth of the fire and continued his vigil.

Kitty awoke in the throes of a nightmare. She'd lost her way in the darkness. Something fierce and dangerous was following her. She started running and lost her footing. In that instant something strong and powerful began attacking her, beating her about the head and shoulders, sending pain crashing through her again and again. She tried to lift her arms to protect herself, but they were pinned down. The more she struggled to free herself, the more fierce the pain became until she suddenly surfaced, her chest rising and falling with each labored breath.

"Easy now, Kitty. You're having a bad dream."

That voice, so soft, so soothing, had her opening her eyes.

Bo was kneeling beside her, cradling her in his arms. His face was so close to hers, she could feel the warmth of his breath on her temple.

"The stallion…?"

"In the corral."

"I made it home?"

He nodded. "Though I don't know how, considering how much pain you must have been suffering."

"It was…bad." Her throat was so dry she could hardly get the words out.

"Would you like something?"

"Water."

He laid her down gently and walked away. While he was gone, Kitty probed her wounds, and felt the binding at her arm and chest. Though her shoulder ached, there was no dressing there.

"Here." Bo lifted her head and held a dipper of water to her lips.

She sighed as the cool water soothed her parched throat. She watched him set the dipper aside. "Who patched me up?"

"I did."

"What's the damage?"

"A broken arm. Some ribs. Your shoulder was separated. Aaron and I snapped it into place."

She nodded, remembering the searing pain that had sent her over the edge.

"My head aches."

"Some of that's probably from the stallion's attack. But a good part of it is probably Aaron's elixir."

"He gave me some of that?" She wrinkled her nose.

"I have to admit, it seemed to help. And you were awfully talkative when it started to take effect."

"Talkative?" She shot him a killing look. "What did I say?"

"Only that you thought I was handsome. Or as you called it, pretty."

She could see the grin he was trying to hide. "I hope you're not going to take the word of a drunk."

"You mean you don't think I'm good-looking?"

"What you are, Bo Chandler, is arrogant, annoying, and smug."

"Guilty on all counts. But you're evading the question, Kitty. Do you find me attractive?"

"I find you...offensive."

He merely smiled. "Are you in any pain?"

His sudden change of subject had her looking at him with suspicion. "Yes. Why?"

"Aaron left instructions that I was to give you more elixir if you complained of any pain."

She was already shaking her head. "I'd have to be at death's door to take another swallow of that swill."

"Coward. You're just afraid that once you're under the influence of that whiskey, you'll slip and tell me something else you don't want me to know."

She could feel the color flooding her cheeks. "I don't like losing control of my senses for any reason."

He tucked the furs around her neck, allowing his hands to linger there a moment. Without giving a thought to what he was doing, he leaned close to brush a kiss over her cheek. "In the future I'll keep that in mind."

She absorbed the quick rush of heat, and the slow tingling that seemed to go all the way to her toes.

"See that you do. And see that…" The flush on her cheeks deepened. "…you leave the rest of my shirt on me. As it is, I'm barely dressed."

"I left the…essentials modestly covered."

He saw the flash of temper in her eyes before the lashes fluttered closed. She was asleep almost instantly.

Bo stretched out on the rug beside her, watching her while she slept. He didn't know if his presence beside her would do anything to ease her pain, but it would go a long way toward easing his.

When he'd first seen her, pale and wounded, he'd been afraid his heart would simply shut down and refuse to beat. He had no doubt it would have if her wounds had been more serious. Now, seeing her snug and warm and safe, he had the almost over-whelming desire to gather her into his arms and hold her close, so that he could hear the sound of her breathing, and feel the steady beat of her pulse.

Instead, he had to content himself with merely looking at her. It was, he thought, like having a glimpse of heaven.

Chapter Eight

Kitty lay, eyes closed, feeling the warmth of the morning sun streaming through the cabin window. It took her a moment to realize she wasn't lying in her sleeping loft, but rather on the floor, near the fire. Her body ached in a dozen different places, and her head felt heavy. But it was neither the pain nor the discomfort that had wakened her. She had the distinct impression that she was being watched.

She opened her eyes to find Bo lying beside her, his eyes steady on hers. It was the strangest feeling.

She lifted a hand to the tangle of hair in her eyes. "Did you sleep at all?"

"Some. How do you feel?"

"Sore."

"Would you like some coffee?"

She shook her head. "I don't think so."

"Eggs? Biscuits?"

"Maybe later." She didn't try to sit up, knowing it would bring more pain. Instead she lay quietly, wishing he would turn away from her. The way he was staring at her sent shivers along her spine. "Have you been here all night?"

He nodded. "I figured you might wake and need something."

"You didn't need to stay close. I could have called out."

"I didn't mind. I liked being here beside you, watching you sleep."

"Well, I..." She couldn't think of anything sensible to say, and was relieved to see Aaron's door open. She turned to watch the old man limping across the room.

He stopped beside her and took in the scene in silence.

Bo rolled to his side and got up, heading across the room toward the kitchen table. "I'll have coffee ready in a while."

"No hurry." Aaron eased himself into the chair and studied Kitty. "How're you feeling, girl?"

"Sore. But I'll live."

"That you will." He managed a shaky laugh. "You had us scared last night."

"Sorry, Aaron."

He was already holding up a hand. "You've got nothing to be sorry about. You did all the right things. And you made it home. That's all that matters.''

"I wasn't sure if I could, but I was bound to try."
She smiled up at him. "You'll never know how good this old place looked to me."

"I think I do. I've been in your boots a time or two, girl. When the world turns against you, there's nothing like coming home."

"Yeah." She gave a sigh of disgust. "I really made a muddle of things. Looks like I won't be breaking that herd of mustangs to saddle for a while."

Bo looked up from the pot of coffee he'd set to boiling over the fire. "Maybe I could give it a try."

"You?" Kitty couldn't hide the note of sarcasm in her voice. "What would you know about breaking mustangs?"

"I guess I won't know until I try. But I grew up around horses. I don't see that there could be much difference between a mustang and a skittish Thoroughbred."

Kitty and Aaron exchanged knowing glances.

It was the old man who said, "You might want to give this some thought, son. These are wild critters. You saw what that stallion did to Kitty. And she's been around them all her life."

Bo nodded. "I'm no fool, Aaron. I'm not going to go charging into that corral thinking I can break him in a day. But I'd like to at least see what I can do."

The old man shrugged. "It's your bones that'll be broken if you fail. And your backside that'll take the punishment, even if you succeed."

"Then you don't mind if I try?"

Aaron shook his head. "Not at all."

Bo turned to Kitty. "This is your herd. What do you say?"

She yawned and snuggled into the fur nest. "Do whatever you want. I'm betting by this time tomorrow you'll wish you'd never seen that mustang stallion. But before you deal with him, you'd better round up his herd of mares and get them into the holding pen before they start to stray."

"I'll get at it right after breakfast." Smiling, Bo returned his attention to a batch of biscuit dough.

From his position on the chair, Aaron found himself wondering which of these two young people to feel sorrier for; the feisty little female who probably wouldn't be able to sit a horse for weeks, or the man with the soft hands who was about to get his bones rattled.

It was late afternoon by the time Bo had managed to round up all the mares and secure them in the holding pen. Using Kitty's horse and lasso, he worked up a sweat chasing them across hills and fields. He was amazed at how determined they were to elude capture. He was just as determined to see that every one of them was accounted for, if only to prove to Kitty that her injury hadn't been in vain.

Once inside the small corral, the herd milled about, rearing, bucking, snorting their displeasure at being separated from the stallion. For his part, the stallion thrashed about in the isolation corral, his hooves crashing against the rail fence that held him prisoner.

Through it all Aaron sat on the porch where he could hear Kitty calling if she should wake. From this vantage point he could see that Bo was no novice to handling horseflesh. The mustang mares used every trick they knew to evade his rope, but in the end, Bo managed to bring them all in.

Aaron looked up when the door opened and Kitty, wrapped in a blanket, stood leaning weakly in the doorway.

"You shouldn't be up, girl."

"Why not?"

"Because you need to rest and heal."

"I've rested all I can today." She'd been lying in her bedroll, too sore to get up, yet too curious to stay abed. In the end, curiosity won.

She craned her neck. "Is Bo still off chasing the mares?"

Aaron nodded in the direction of the pen. ''He brought the last of them in a while ago.''

Surprised, Kitty walked unsteadily out onto the porch and sat wearily down on the step. As she did, she caught sight of Bo as he let himself inside the gate of the isolation corral. He carefully latched it behind him, then turned and approached the stallion. He appeared to be talking as he held out a bridle for the animal to sniff.

The mustang stood perfectly still, nostrils flared, ears flattened.

Kitty leaned forward, hands on her knees, watching intently. ''I hope he knows that it isn't the scent of leather that has that stallion spooked, it's the scent of man.''

''I expect he'll soon find that out for himself.''

As Bo approached, the horse began backing up until, reaching the bars of the corral, it reared up, hooves slashing the air.

''Fool,'' Kitty muttered under her breath.

The stallion danced sideways, then began running in circles around the corral, always just missing Bo, who stood his ground. This went on for an hour or more, with the horse racing straight toward Bo, then shying away at the last moment.

Bo stood perfectly still, always making eye contact with the stallion as it charged forward. He could feel the whistle of wind as the animal flew past him, sending dirt from its hooves thick enough to clog his lungs and cloud his vision.

He knew this game. Had played it dozens of times with the high-strung Thoroughbreds on his grandfather's Virginia farm. Each spring the new batch of yearlings would test the men whose task it was to make them comfortable with riders. The scent of leather, the restrictions of saddle and bridle, and the added burden of a human on their backs, sent them into a frenzy.

With this creature of the wild, there was an additional challenge. Trust. Or rather, the lack of it. Living free in the hills, the mustang had never felt the touch of a man's hand. Had never been fed by man. Owed his allegiance to no man.

Finally, as the sun began to dip behind the peaks of the Black Hills, the stallion began to tire of the game. Choosing a spot that was as far away from Bo as possible, the animal stood perfectly still, watching and listening.

"Time for supper. Yours and mine. But we'll see to yours first." Bo kept his eyes fixed on the horse as he backed out of the corral. Using a pitchfork he tossed hay over the rail and dumped a bucket of water into a trough.

He watched with satisfaction as the mustang took a step forward. Only a step, but it was enough.

Bo turned away, smiling. He was still smiling

when he caught sight of Kitty and Aaron seated on the porch. "You're up. A good sign. How's the arm feel?"

"Sore." She gave a nod toward the corral. "What was that all about? I thought you were going to break him to saddle."

"First things first. He knows my scent now. And the sound of my voice. By this time tomorrow, I expect he'll allow me to touch him."

"Just like that?" Kitty shot a glance at Aaron. But instead of the laughter she'd anticipated, the old man looked intrigued.

"Well." Bo plunged his arms into the bucket of fresh water he'd left on the porch, dumping more water over his head and face before snatching up a clean towel. "Guess I'd better think about something for supper."

Aaron gave a guilty start. "I'm really sorry, son. I guess Kitty and I got so caught up in watching you, we forgot about food."

"Don't worry. There's enough beef and biscuits left. I can have them ready in no time." He walked away whistling, leaving Aaron and Kitty to stare after him in surprise.

It was clear that Bo Chandler was as laid-back handling mustangs as he was fixing a good meal. Which only made him more of a puzzle than ever.

Aaron sat back, sipping a second cup of coffee, and nibbling on his third biscuit. "You looked like you were enjoying yourself with that ornery herd today, son."

"I was. It felt good to be in the saddle again. It's been a while. I've missed it." Bo glanced at Kitty. "I see you're still wrapped up in that blanket. You feeling cold?"

She looked away, avoiding his eyes. "Not exactly. But I couldn't get myself dressed."

"What was I thinking?" Bo scraped back his chair. "Do you keep your clothes up in the loft?"

"What clothes?"

He turned to study her. "The rest of your clothes. You do have more than one set of buckskins, don't you?" The moment the words were out of his mouth he regretted them. He could tell, by the flush on her cheeks, that he'd hit a nerve. "It doesn't matter." He lifted a hand when she tried to interrupt. "You'd never get that bandaged arm through the sleeve. " He picked up one of his own shirts and held it out to her. "I'll hold the blanket while you put your good arm in this sleeve."

She did as he suggested, then grasped the lapels of the shirt together for the sake of modesty.

He lowered the blanket and began buttoning the front of the shirt.

With each press of his fingers she felt a jolt

through her system. Glancing up, she saw him pause to meet her eyes. At once she looked away, only to find Aaron watching them both. That only made her all the more aware of the heat that stained her cheeks.

When Bo had finished the last button he left the empty sleeve to dangle at her side. ''There now. Another problem solved. Isn't that easier than holding a blanket around you all day?''

''A whole lot easier.'' She turned away so quickly she nearly stumbled. ''Thanks.''

''You're welcome. Why don't you and Aaron go sit by the fire while I clean up here?''

Kitty didn't argue. She was feeling far too shaky, and blaming it on her injuries. It certainly wasn't because of the intimacy of Bo Chandler's touch. But when she settled herself in a chair near the fire, she could see Aaron still looking at her in the way he had when he was puzzling over something she'd said or done.

Suddenly she could feel the walls of the tiny cabin closing in on her. Before, when that happened, she could always climb to her loft and lose herself in dreaming. Since she wasn't strong enough to attempt the ladder, she had no other choice but to head for the door.

''Where're you going, girl?''

She pushed open the door. ''Just out. Maybe I'll

take a turn around the corral, and take a look at the new herd.''

"Want some company?''

Without turning around she called, "I'll be fine, Aaron. I won't be long.''

Once outside she made it as far as the corral before leaning weakly on the rail. The stallion stood on the far side looking like a shadow in the darkness. He gave a whinny to his mares, and the herd in the next corral shifted nervously.

Kitty lifted her head and studied the path of a shooting star.

"You're supposed to make a wish.''

At the sound of Bo's voice she whirled to find him standing directly behind her. "What are you doing here?''

"Keeping an eye on you." Seeing the sudden flash of fire in her eyes he held up his hands in defense. "It wasn't my idea. I'm here on orders from Aaron. He thinks you're too weak to be out here alone.''

"I'm fine.''

"Yes, you are." His voice lowered to a whisper. He lifted a finger to her cheek. Just the softest touch, but it had her heart thundering. "You're just about the finest woman I've ever met, Kitty.''

"Don't…''

"Kiss you?" He shook his head. "I don't want

to take advantage of your weakness. But I just have to taste those lips again. Just one taste.''

He kept his eyes steady on hers as he lowered his head and brushed his mouth over hers. As he'd promised, it was just a touch, but it had them both reacting as though burned.

Kitty stepped back. As though anticipating her reaction, his hand was already at her back, his other hand in her hair, cupping the back of her head. ''I was wrong.'' His eyes gleamed in the darkness, and she could see the flash of his quick smile. ''One taste isn't nearly enough.''

His mouth covered hers in a kiss so hungry, she forgot to breathe. As he took the kiss deeper, her heart forgot to beat. And then it started thundering like a herd of stampeding cattle.

She'd intended to pull away. But the moment his mouth found hers, she was lost in the wonder of it. The quick jittery pulse that shot through her veins, heating her blood, clouding her mind. The liquid warmth that had her skin damp, her bones soft and pliant. And that hard knot of desire that settled deep inside her.

Bo lingered over her lips, loving the taste of her, the feel of her here in his arms. He could feel the press of her breasts through the thin fabric of his shirt. Could feel the way her nipples hardened. He couldn't resist running his hands along her sides until his thumbs encountered the soft swell of her breasts. He felt the way she flinched, but as he took the kiss deeper, she forgot her fear as she lost herself in him.

There was so much pleasure here. Just having her in his arms, her mouth warm and willing on his, had his mind emptying of every thought except her. He knew he was taking advantage of her weakness. But right now, this moment, all he could think of was the way her erratic heartbeat kept time to his, telling him she was as caught up in the pleasure as he.

"Kitty. Bo." Aaron's voice calling from the porch had their heads coming up sharply. "You two out there?"

Bo kept his hands at her shoulders, as much for himself as for her, while he shouted, "We're at the corral, Aaron." His voice was low and deep in the darkness.

"You two had better come inside, before Kitty catches a chill."

"All right." Keeping his arm around her shoulders Bo led her toward the figure on the porch.

Kitty was grateful for his strength. The truth was, her legs felt as if they might turn to rubber at any moment. And her heartbeat was still so erratic, she felt as though she were floating.

As they climbed the steps Aaron asked, "You all right?"

"I'm fine, Aaron. But I think I'll turn in now."

The old man reached into his pocket. "Thought I'd sit a spell and enjoy a cigar. Care to join me, Bo?"

"Thanks." Bo accepted the cigar from Aaron's hand and leaned close while the old man held a match to the tip.

As they sat smoking in the darkness, Bo thought about the woman inside the cabin, getting ready for bed. And found himself wondering just how much longer he could go on being this close to her while continuing to deny the desire that flared each time they touched.

Chapter Nine

'' '' Morning, girl.'' Aaron looked up from his seat on the porch as Kitty paused in the doorway. ''How're you feeling?''

''Miserable.'' It had become her standard response in the past few days. And it was true. As her wounds began to heal, her usually sunny, upbeat spirit plummeted. She missed her bed in the loft. Missed getting into her clothes in the morning and heading out to see to her chores. And she absolutely hated having to ask for help with things that had once been so easy. In the past couple of days she'd left her hair hanging in her eyes rather than struggle to tie it back with the length of rawhide she usually used. She'd gone without a bath down in the creek. Gone without a change of clothes, choosing instead to wear Bo's shirt over her buckskin britches. She'd even taken to going barefoot rather than face the struggle of getting into her boots.

She glanced around. "Something seems different."

Aaron shrugged. "Take your pick. It might be the new steps Bo put in. He said those old ones were ready to collapse any day now. Or it could be this." He pointed to the wooden bench positioned alongside his chair. "With three of us, Bo thought it'd be cozier with more seats out here." He patted the bench. "Go ahead. Try it."

She frowned as she sat down, testing her weight against the sturdy wooden back. "How's Bo coming with that stallion?"

"See for yourself."

She glanced toward the corral and her jaw dropped. "He's riding him?"

"You bet. In fact, Bo says that stallion took to the saddle so easily, he can't wait to tackle the mares."

Kitty's frown deepened. "If my arm doesn't heal soon, he'll have the entire herd saddled and ready to sell before I've done a lick of work with them."

"That wouldn't be the worst thing to happen, girl. Look at all the money you'll have when they're sold."

"Yeah." She stared hard at the toe of her boot, wondering at the gloom that seemed to have settled over her like a dark cloud.

"If you'd like some breakfast, Bo left you biscuits and beef."

"Do you hear yourself, Aaron? Bo fixed the steps. Bo made us a new bench. Bo cooked breakfast. Is there anything Bo can't do?"

Aaron glanced over. "Maybe you ought to go back to bed for a while."

She got up so quickly pain jolted through her arm, causing her to let loose. "I'm not some dog-eared, flea-bitten old mule about to roll over and die from a few broken bones, Aaron. Stop treating me like I am."

The old man got slowly to his feet, leaning heavily on his cane. With his hand on her arm he fixed her with a puzzled look. "What's eating at you, Kitty?"

"It's this." She touched a hand to the sling that held her arm. "I'm not sick enough to stay in bed any longer. But with my arm like this, I can't do any of the things I want to do. Oh, Aaron, I feel so useless."

"You, Kitty? With all the things you do?"

"Name one thing I've done in the past week?"

He shook his head. "You're mending, girl. In no time you'll be feeling like your old self again." He gave her a gentle smile. "Until then, why not just enjoy this change in your routine? Go ahead inside and help yourself to the food Bo fixed you." He saw the way her eyes flashed and added quickly, ''Then come back out here and sit a spell. We'll watch that tenderfoot kiss the dirt a couple of times when he tries to put a saddle on that dappled mare.''

That had her smiling as she walked inside. A short time later she returned to the porch. But each time Bo was thrown from the saddle, though she shared a laugh with Aaron, she felt an odd little jolt around her heart.

It was a feeling she didn't care for. And one that had her much more troubled than she was willing to admit.

''Here, Kitty.'' Bo, his face freshly washed, his hair glistening with droplets of water, rounded the table and paused beside her chair. ''I'll cut that meat for you.''

''I can cut it myself.'' She pulled the plate away when he reached for it.

''All right. Suit yourself.'' He was whistling as he filled their cups with coffee.

While he and Aaron bent to their supper, Kitty sat wallowing in misery. She resented the fact that the cabin smelled so good. Bo had scrubbed every inch of it until it gleamed. The windows were so clean the sunlight was streaming through them like torches. He'd even carried everything down from her sleeping loft, hanging her fur throws and blankets on a line in the spring sunshine while he dumped buckets of hot soapy water over everything. What was even worse, he'd done it all with such good humor. It seemed the more miserable she felt, the sweeter he acted.

For Kitty, the worst thing of all was the way she was feeling. Like a petulant child. But she couldn't seem to climb out of this hole of self-pity. The more Bo did, the deeper grew her gloom.

Aaron nodded toward her plate. "You don't like your beef, girl?"

"It's fine. I'm just not very hungry."

"Force yourself to eat." Aaron broke a biscuit in half and began to mop up his gravy. "It'll help heal your bones."

"Do you know that for a fact, Aaron?" She fixed him with a look that would have shriveled most men's souls. "Or are you just saying that to get me to do something I don't want to do?"

He barely glanced at her. "I haven't seen you this testy since Yale left us without a word."

"That was more than ten years ago."

He nodded. "That's about right. You were a lot younger then, girl. But that pout on your lips looked the same."

"That's it." She shoved back her chair and got to her feet. "I'm going down to the creek."

"Too cold tonight to take a bath. Besides, with

that arm in a sling, you'd probably slip on a rock and knock yourself out cold.''

''What does my arm have to do with my ability to walk through a stream?''

''Makes you clumsy. You'd best wait until you're healed.''

''That does it.'' She slammed out of the cabin, turning the air blue with a string of curses.

When she was gone Bo studied the old man's bowed head. ''You just going to let her go?''

''Let her? Do you hear yourself, son? With that ornery little female, there's no such thing as letting her do anything. Kitty has always done exactly what she pleases. And woe to anyone who tries to tell her otherwise.''

''What's behind all this sudden temper, Aaron?''

The old man shrugged. ''She's watching you doing all her chores, and doing some of them better'n she ever did, and it hurts. She told me she's feeling useless. Of course, that's not the whole truth. She's just feeling sorry for herself. She's not used to doing nothing. It just doesn't sit well with her. I suppose like all females, she needs a little pampering.''

''I see.'' Bo leaned back, staring at the last rays of sunlight spilling across the floor of the cabin. At length he said, ''I think I might know something that could help.''

He filled several buckets with water and put them

over the fire. While they were heating, he moved about the cabin, laying out several soft squares of linen.

As evening shadows began to settle over the land, they heard Kitty's footsteps on the porch. She stepped inside and looked around in puzzlement.

"What's this?"

"You said you wanted a bath. Aaron and I will go sit on the porch for a spell so you can have the cabin to yourself. But before you do, I'll wash your hair."

"You'll…wash my hair?" She glanced at Aaron, and realized that he looked as surprised as she.

"You can't do it with just one arm." Bo grinned. "And I happen to have two arms that work just fine." He motioned toward the tub of steaming water. "Just kneel over here by the fire and let me do the rest."

"I don't need any help, thank you."

"I know you don't, Kitty. But I want to help you." He steered her toward the tub of water and urged her down beside it.

Before she knew what she was doing, Kitty was kneeling with her head bent over the side of the tub, allowing Bo Chandler to lather up her hair. "If you think I'm going to…" The protest died in her throat the minute his fingers began massaging her scalp. It was the most purely sensual feeling she'd ever experienced.

"Watch that you don't get that arm wet." He lifted the dipper and began pouring water over her soapy hair, all the while running his fingers through the tangles.

Such strong fingers, she realized. She'd once thought of his hands as soft. But they were surprisingly strong, as well. And causing the most amazing feelings gliding like warm honey down her spine.

It occurred to Bo that he was having himself a fine time. It was just about the sweetest torture of his life to run his fingers through her hair, and not be able to do more. But he could see Aaron watching them, and knew he had to behave himself. Still, though he may have told her he was merely helping her, the truth was, he'd been itching to touch her like this, and he now had the perfect excuse. He knew he was taking advantage of her weakness, but he told himself it was for her own good.

"How does that feel?" Her hair was even softer than he'd anticipated. Softer than the muzzle of a newborn calf. With every touch, his fingertips tingled.

"It's…fine. Just fine." She fell silent, too steeped in pleasure to speak.

Because he didn't want the moment to end, he soaped her hair again, taking his time massaging her scalp before rinsing the soap. One look at her face told him what she would never admit to. Though she'd resisted, she was now thoroughly enjoying herself.

Almost as much as he was.

He wrapped a towel around her hair before helping her to her feet. "Would you like me to unbutton that shirt?"

"Yes, I'd…" She blinked, abruptly pulling herself back to reality. "No. I can manage by myself."

"All right." He indicated a long, flowing gown draped over the back of a chair. "When you're finished with your bath, you might want to slip into that. It'd be a lot simpler than trying to get dressed."

Kitty frowned. "What is that?"

He shrugged. "Just something I found in an old carpetbag up in your loft. I washed everything in it and hung them out to dry."

"My ma's things." Kitty ran a hand over the gown. "That was her dressing gown. I remember seeing her in it when I was little. I'd have thought by now it would be falling apart."

He shook his head. "It seemed just fine to me." He turned away with a knowing smile. "Aaron and I will be outside if you need us for anything."

The old man eased himself out of his chair and removed two cigars from his pocket. "It looks like a good night for sitting and smoking, son."

As he held the door, Bo glanced back at Kitty, who was standing perfectly still, watching him.

"Take as long as you want. Don't worry. We won't disturb you."

But he did, she realized. He did disturb her, every time he got too close.

With a sigh she fumbled with the buttons of the shirt, then stripped off her buckskin leggings. Climbing into the warm water, she gave a sigh of pure pleasure.

Leaning her head back, she closed her eyes and let the soap and the water and the peacefulness of the moment weave their magic.

Or was it the image of Bo Chandler, kneeling over her, massaging her scalp, that created the magic?

Whatever the answer, her black mood seemed to have lifted considerably. Lying here in warm, scented water, hearing the hum of low, masculine voices out on the porch as Bo and Aaron talked and smoked in the darkness, it was impossible to hold on to the gloom.

She glanced over at her mother's old dressing gown and came to a decision. When she was finished with her bath she would wash the shirt and buckskin leggings, and let them dry overnight by the fire. She supposed it wouldn't hurt to wear something silly and feminine for just one night. And tomorrow, no matter how awkward she was with only one good arm, she was going to resume as many of her activities as possible.

She sank deeper into the water and felt a smile tug at her lips.

Amazing.

Who would have believed that something as simple as a warm bath in front of the fire could so completely change her attitude? Right now she felt as if she could tame an entire herd of mustangs single-handedly. She glanced down at her arm in the sling and chuckled. She might have only one good arm, but she still had her wits about her. There must be dozens of things she could do with one hand.

First thing tomorrow morning she'd find out for herself.

Chapter Ten

"I saw you take a couple of nasty spills from that mare today, son." Aaron drew on his cigar and watched a wreath of smoke curl over his head. "How's your backside feeling?"

"Tender." Bo grinned. "But she's coming around. I figure another day and I'll be ready to start on another one."

"I've been watching you. You're a natural."

"Thanks." Bo's smile grew. "I wasn't so sure of that when I first started. You and Kitty were right about mustangs. They're a different breed from Thoroughbreds. A lot more cagey and clever, though I suppose they have to be to survive in the wild."

Aaron nodded. "They've learned to deal with all kinds of weather. Heat and drought that dry up the prairie grass as well as the streams and rivers. And snowstorms that can trap them in canyons with no food and no way to escape for weeks on end."

"I wonder what they think when they find themselves in warm barns with enough food to last them an entire winter." It occurred to Bo that they could have been talking about Kitty when she'd first arrived here at Aaron's cabin. After the nightmare existence she'd survived, it must have looked like pure heaven. "I suppose they're skittish for..." Bo's words died as the door opened and Kitty paused in the doorway. She looked so incredible in the white dressing gown, her hair a tangle of curls tumbling to her waist. Like an angel that had just dropped down to earth.

"You can come inside now." She turned away. "I'm finished with my bath."

Bo knew his mouth was open, but he couldn't close it. He was grateful when Aaron answered for both of them.

"We'll be right in, girl." Aaron took a last draw on his cigar before carefully stubbing it out on the porch railing. He turned to Bo, who was still staring at the now-empty doorway. "You coming, son?"

"Hmm?" Bo glanced down at his hand to see that Aaron was taking the cigar from him so he wouldn't burn his hand.

He followed the old man inside the cabin, where it was warm and steamy. Kitty's buckskin leggings and his shirt were hanging over the backs of chairs positioned in front of the fire. Kitty seemed unaware of the fact that her dressing gown, in the light of the lantern, revealed every line and curve of that lithe young body beneath.

She turned with a smile. "I feel wonderful. Thank you, Bo. That was just what I needed."

"You're welcome." He hadn't moved since he'd stepped inside. He couldn't. His feet were frozen to the spot as he studied the way she looked.

He'd once seen a painting of a fictional goddess trapped in a castle who had let down her long hair for her lover. No fictional creature had ever looked as lovely as this flesh-and-blood woman. A woman who had no idea of the effect of her own beauty.

Kitty indicated the tub of cooling water. "If you two would like to toss that, I'd be grateful."

Aaron moved to the tub, then glanced toward Bo, who was watching Kitty cross to the fire to warm herself. "You care to give me a hand, son?"

Bo blinked, then hurried to Aaron's side. "I'll take care of this, Aaron. You just sit down."

The old man did, watching as Bo hauled the tub of water out the door. Minutes later, when he returned, Aaron watched as he set the tub in a corner of the room before crossing to Kitty, who was running a brush through her hair.

His voice had grown considerably softer. "Need any help with that?"

At his question she looked up and gave him a

smile. "No, thanks, Bo. I can manage. You've done enough."

"I don't mind." He was close enough to breathe her in. His hand clenched at his side before he took the brush from her and began running it through the tangles.

Each movement had his throat going dry and all the blood rushing to his loins.

Kitty found herself fighting the most amazing sensations. Her heart was doing the strangest things in her chest. And her mind was actually spinning in dizzying circles with each touch of the brush to her hair.

She glanced at her bedroll, lying on the rug. "I think I'm going to have to turn in soon. That warm water made me sleepy."

"I'm...feeling a bit tired myself." Bo tossed aside the hairbrush and tucked his bedroll under his arm, prepared to spread it out beside hers.

Just then Aaron, who'd been watching the two of them, pulled himself out of his chair. "I've been thinking..." He cleared his throat and waited until Bo and Kitty gave him their attention. "I've been thinking that maybe it's about time you made up a place for yourself in the barn, Bo. There's a clean, empty stall out there. The nights are warmer now. And as long as Kitty can't climb up to her loft, it's getting a bit crowded in here with the three of us."

Kitty closed her eyes a moment against a nearly overpowering urge to resist. Then her mind cleared a bit and she realized just how foolishly she'd been behaving. Like some sort of silly female.

"That's a fine idea, Aaron." The more she thought about it, the more she realized it was the perfect solution. Some distance between herself and Bo was exactly what she needed.

She seemed actually relieved as she turned to Bo. "What do you think?"

He gave a reluctant nod of his head. "I don't know what I was thinking of. I should have suggested it long before this." He studied Kitty for a moment longer, before turning toward the door. "I'll say good-night now. I'll see you both in the morning."

Seeing that his hands were full Kitty hurried across the room and held the door.

As he stepped onto the porch she touched a hand to his arm. Just a touch, but it started a surge of heat racing through her veins. At once she lowered her hand to her side. "Good night, Bo. I hope you sleep well."

"You, too." His gaze centered on her mouth, and he felt the jolt as surely as if he'd already tasted those lips. When he finally managed to look away he called, "'Night, Aaron."

"Good night, Bo."

The old man saw the way Kitty lingered in the doorway until Bo's figure disappeared into the darkness. When she turned, he knew, by the look on her face, that he'd been right in his assumption.

These two might not know it yet, but they were both fighting a mighty strong attraction. And though Bo might be enjoying himself in these first stages of puppy love, Aaron couldn't tell from Kitty's eyes whether she was ecstatically happy or scared to death.

It was time he had a talk with Bo Chandler.

Aaron knew he wasn't blood kin to Kitty, but he was the next best thing. Somebody had to look out for her interest.

"I think I'll go help Bo get settled in the barn." He leaned on his cane as he limped to the door. "No need for you to wait up."

Bo dropped his bedroll on the fresh straw before leaning an arm on the top rail on the stall and glancing around. Part of him was relieved that there'd been a clearer head than his in that cabin. There was no telling where it might have ended otherwise. Still, another part of him felt thoroughly frustrated. Kitty had looked so damnably alluring, he'd wanted to stay there the night and just look at her.

He gave a snort of laughter. Who was he kidding? He'd wanted to devour her right there on the spot.

He had no doubt that as soon as Aaron had gone to his bedroom, leaving them alone, he'd have tried to seduce her. And that look in her eyes wasn't so hard to read. After that long lazy bath she was feeling as contented as a kitten and ready to be cuddled.

He was just the man to do it. In truth, he ached to hold her.

He looked up as the barn door was thrust open and Aaron stepped inside, closing the door behind him.

"Did I forget something, Aaron?"

"No, son. I did."

Bo studied him as he limped across the floor and paused beside the stall. "I thought I ought to tell you a little about Kitty."

"She told me about her childhood journey here. And the fact that you made a home for her and her brothers. She's grown into a fine woman, Aaron."

"That she has." The old man settled himself on a bale of hay, carefully setting his cane aside. "It hasn't been easy for her to be raised in a man's world. When she first came to me, I didn't know quite what to do with one small, helpless female."

"Helpless?" Bo threw back his head and laughed.

Aaron joined him. "I'll admit, she isn't like most females. But in certain ways, she is." He shook his head. "I could teach her a lot about ranching and breaking mustangs. But there was one thing I couldn't teach her.'' He looked down at his gnarled hands. "How to be a female. The first time her…" He flushed. "…monthly arrived, she came flying into the cabin telling me she must have hurt herself. I put her in the wagon and drove her to Misery so Doc Honeywell could have a look at her. Poor Doc had to tell her the facts of life. Afterward he ordered me to haul her over to Swensen's Dry Goods so Inga Swensen could explain what females needed to do each month." The old man looked over at Bo. "I've never told another soul that story, son. And I'm telling you because…" He chose his words carefully. "I see the way you look at her. And I think you ought to know that, growing up on a ranch, Kitty knows all about what happens between animals. But she's not quite sure about how it's done with men and women. Living way out here, she's been isolated from other females. She's never been to a town dance or social. Never even kissed a boy that I know of. So she's…" He searched for a word to describe Kitty. "She's…tender." He fixed Bo with a look. "I couldn't stand to see her hurt."

Bo nodded. "I understand. And I appreciate you telling me this, Aaron."

"Then you see why you have to sleep out here now? And why you'll have to treat her with some…care?"

"I do. I can't promise you that she won't be hurt.

But I can give you my word, Aaron, that I'll do everything in my power to see that I'm not the one to cause her any pain.''

''That's all I ask, son.'' Aaron offered his hand.

The two men shook hands.

When the old man had gone, Bo lay in his bedroll, his hands under his head, and thought about all that Aaron had told him.

Suddenly his lips curved into a grin.

That sly old fox.

He'd not only painted Kitty as every man's fantasy woman. Sweet. Untouched. Innocent. He'd also made it impossible for Bo to seduce her, without breaking his word.

He felt that he'd just been backed into a small, tight corner. With no way out.

''What are you doing?'' Aaron looked up in time to see Kitty poke a stick under the linen that was wrapped around her arm and begin to scratch.

''I'm itching something fierce.''

She and the old man were leaning on the rails of the corral, watching while Bo eased a saddle on the back of a skittish mare.

''If you break the skin you could get that wound dirty. Then you'd have all kinds of problems, girl.''

''I can't help it. I'd just about tear off my arm to stop this itching.''

"That does it." He cupped his hands around his mouth and called to Bo, "Son, I think it's time you took Kitty into town to see Doc Honeywell."

Beside him she gave a hiss of anger. "I don't need a doctor."

He arched a brow. "That's what you said the time I patched you up after you got yourself tangled in barbed wire. Doc told me later that if we'd waited much longer, you'd have died of blood poisoning."

"Well, I'm not dying now. I'm just scratching."

"And I say it's time to have the doc take a look at that arm." He turned to shout, and found Bo standing right beside him. He gave a sheepish grin. "There you are. I think you and Kitty both need a break from ranch chores. How about taking her into town? She can let Doc Honeywell take a look at that arm, and while you're there you might be able to sell a couple of these mustangs and pick up the supplies we need."

Bo wiped his sleeve across his damp forehead. "Sounds good to me." He glanced at Kitty. "I can be ready to leave in a few minutes."

She had that familiar pout on her lips. "I'm not going."

He grinned. "All right. I guess I can sell the mustangs by myself. How much do you think they're worth, Aaron?"

Her eyes flashed. "Why are you asking him?

They're my mustangs. And I'll be the one to say what they're worth.''

He shrugged. ''Suit yourself. Give me a price, and I'll try to fetch it for you.''

''I can sell them myself.'' She started toward the cabin. ''I'll just get my hat and I'll be ready to go.''

As she flounced away, Aaron turned to Bo with a grin. ''That was real clever of you, son. I figured we were going to have a battle on our hands getting her to town.''

Bo laughed. ''My father used to tell me there was always more than one way to persuade a judge or jury.''

''Then I'd say you were paying attention.'' Aaron started toward the cabin. ''I'll put together a list of supplies.''

''You're not going with us?''

The old man shook his head. ''There was a time when it didn't seem like much of a trek. But these days I can't sit a horse. And the minute that wagon starts its jarring, this old leg throbs like the fires of hell.''

As he limped away, Bo started off in the direction of the creek. He figured he'd better make himself presentable for his first appearance in the town of Misery.

Chapter Eleven

Aaron and Kitty were standing on the front porch when Bo brought the horse and cart from the barn. He stopped at the corral and tied the stallion and two mares to the back of the cart before proceeding toward the cabin.

As Bo leaped to the ground Kitty couldn't help staring. He'd washed in the creek, and his dark hair, badly in need of a trim, still glistened with drops of water. He'd changed into a clean white shirt and his black jacket. She was reminded again of the stranger he'd been when first they'd met. There had been about him a look of danger. And more than a little mystery.

"Kitty and I went over the things we need." Aaron remained on the porch as Kitty walked toward the cart.

Before she could attempt to pull herself up to the

seat, Bo was beside her, lifting her in his arms in one smooth movement.

She felt the jolt to her system and struggled not to react as he settled her on the hard seat.

He climbed up beside her and took up the reins. "With any luck, we should be back by dark, Aaron."

A flick of the reins had the horse leaning into the harness. As they rolled away, Kitty turned and waved to the old man.

When she turned back, her smile faded. "I wish Aaron could go with us. He used to enjoy his visits to town."

Bo glanced over, hearing the sadness in her tone. "If you bought one of those big fancy carriages he could manage the trip."

She gave a laugh. "Oh, I'll do that. Just as soon as I discover gold in the creek."

He gave her a heart-stopping smile. "Stranger things have been known to happen."

She shook her head, sending her golden curls dancing. "Not to us."

"How can you say that? Didn't you tell me your brothers and you had just begun to give up hope of ever seeing civilization again before you stumbled onto Aaron's land?"

She shrugged. "That's true. But I guess one miracle is all anyone can hope for in a lifetime."

"Oh, I don't know about that." He shot her a knowing look. "Where to first?"

"Jeb Simmons's ranch. It's out of the way, but I owe him a horse, and he's not one to ever forgive a debt."

"Most people don't."

"True enough. But Jeb's worse than most. He'd like to own half the Dakota Territory by the time he's thirty."

"Then I wish him luck." Bo concentrated on the rocky terrain as he urged the horse along a narrow trail between huge boulders.

When they arrived at the Simmonses' place, Bo watched Kitty sit up very straight, stiffening her spine. Despite her arm in a sling, she looked like a gunfighter about to outdraw her opponent. The thought had him grinning.

A muscular rancher looked up from one of his hog pens, and ambled over to their cart.

"'Bout time you got here." He nodded toward Bo. "Who's this?"

"Bo Chandler, meet Jeb Simmons."

Bo leaned down and offered a handshake.

Jeb hooked a thumb. "Those mustangs broke to saddle?"

Kitty nodded. "They are."

"Do I get my pick?"

She nodded. Seeing the look of greed in his eyes she took her time adding, ''Of the mares.''

His head came up sharply. ''What about the stallion?''

''He's worth a whole lot more than a measly ham or two.''

''You didn't call that ham measly when you and Aaron needed food.''

''Maybe not, but we both know I'd be a fool to let that stallion go for what you'd offer me. So take your pick of the mares and let me get moving. I'm on my way to Misery, where there are plenty of ranchers eager to buy.''

Jeb Simmons looked the mares over carefully, examining their teeth, running a hand over their flanks, lifting their hooves. Finally he caught up the rope holding the spotted mare. ''This one suits me.''

''Fine. But she's worth more than a ham or two.''

''What'll you take for her?''

Kitty pretended to give it some thought before pointing. ''I'm thinking that sow over there.''

Jeb shook his head. ''She's one of my best. Gave me a dozen piglets last spring.''

''Then she's already getting old. You'll have plenty of other sows to replace her. That's my price. Take it or leave it.''

He studied the mare, then gave a reluctant nod of his head. ''Done.''

Kitty smiled. "We'll come by for the sow tomorrow. And I'll expect you to throw in another ham, as well."

He nodded. "You'll have it." He untied the mare, then as an afterthought called, "Nice to meet you, Chandler. Be careful Kitty doesn't relieve you of that fancy coat before she's through."

"I'll keep that in mind, Simmons." With a laugh Bo flicked the reins and the horse and cart moved away.

When they were out of earshot he turned to her with a grin. "You make a fine horse trader, Miss Conover."

"Thank you, Mr. Chandler. I pride myself on it."

He was still laughing as he urged the horse up a steep rise, then paused to gaze at the outline of buildings barely visible in the distance. "Misery?"

She nodded. "I wonder how it will measure up to all those fine cities and towns you've seen across the country."

He held the reins loosely, stretching out his long legs. "One town's pretty much the same as another. It's the people that make it special. Tell me about the people of Misery."

"Well, there's Olaf and Inga Swensen. They own Swensen's Dry Goods. Their son Lars works as a deputy to my brother, Gabe. They're good, hard-working people. And as fair as they come. Then there's Jack Slade, who owns the Red Dog Saloon. That's where my sister-in-law Billie does the cooking.'' She laughed before adding, ''Emma Hardwick runs the town's rescue mission. She's determined to put Jack Slade out of business and save the souls of the women who work for him.''

Bo grinned. ''Sounds like a losing proposition.''

Kitty shrugged. ''I wouldn't know much about that. I've never been inside the Red Dog. But I guess I don't see anything wrong with Jack's women serving drinks to cowboys.''

''Is that what you think they do?''

''Isn't it?'' She glanced over. ''What else is there for them to do?''

Intrigued, Bo tugged on a lock of her hair. ''We'll talk about it another time. Tell me more about the people of Misery.''

Kitty struggled not to shiver at the strange sensations that tingled along her spine at his touch. ''There's Doc Honeywell, who has a surgery in town. And Jesse Cutler. He's skinny as a corral railing, and has a bald head with a fringe of hair all around that reminds me of moss on a stone. He and his wife and six boys run the barbershop and bath. And there's Eli Moffat, who owns the stables. You can't miss him. His middle is so big he can't bend over. His boots are always caked with mud and manure. And he has the biggest hands I've ever seen.

I swear he could pick up a wagon wheel, a half-dozen horseshoes, and a set of harness in one hand, and still have room for more.''

Bo couldn't help laughing at her description. "I'll be sure to notice him.''

Kitty was grinning from ear to ear. "I'm thinking that I've probably forgotten lots of folks, but you'll get to meet them. Almost everybody comes into Swensen's at one time of day or another. I think you'll like most all of them. Except maybe Buck Reedy. Buck has a mean mouth, and he gets a lot meaner when he's drinking, which is most of the time.''

Bo glanced over. "Every town has someone like Buck.''

"Really?''

He nodded. "But as long as the good folks outnumber the bad, the town will survive.''

As they drew near, he saw Kitty's eyes light with pleasure. "You've missed it, haven't you?''

"I guess. Some. I really like being alone out there on Aaron's ranch. But sometimes it's nice to come to town and pass the time with the folks who live here. Especially my brothers and their wives.'' She pointed. "The jail is up at the other end of town. But maybe we ought to stop at Swensen's first, so I can give Inga my order. Then we can go visit with

Gabe and Billie after I have Doc Honeywell take a look at my arm.''

''All right.''

He slowed the horse as they rolled along the dirt track that served as the main street. At the beginning of the town was Eli Moffat's stable. Eli was working the forge, wearing a heavy leather apron, sweat streaming down his face.

When he caught sight of Kitty he lifted a hand in greeting, then, seeing the horses tied behind her rig, beckoned her to stop. He set down the piece of steel he was shaping into a horseshoe.

Kitty put a hand on Bo's arm. ''Looks like Eli might be interested in doing a little horse trading.''

The minute Bo brought the horse and cart to a halt Eli was beside them.

''Hello, Kitty.'' His voice was as gruff as his looks.

''Eli.'' Kitty nodded toward Bo. ''This is Bo Chandler.''

As the two men shook hands, Bo felt his own big hand crushed inside the giant palm.

Eli released his grip to point at the horses behind the cart. ''Those mustangs broke to saddle?''

''They are. Know anyone who's looking to buy?''

''I might be interested. Just sold a plow horse and one of my best mares. What're you asking for them?''

"You can have the mare for fifty dollars. But I'll want a hundred for the stallion. Near as I can tell he's young and strong and will make some cowboy a fine saddle horse."

Eli examined the two horses, then straightened. "I'll give you fifty for the mare, and seventy for the stallion."

"Ninety, Eli. You could breed him and get your money back in one season."

"Eighty, and that's my last offer."

Bo saw the quick frown on Kitty's face as she mentally calculated.

Finally she nodded. "Deal. You can bring the money to Swensen's later. Bo and I are going there now to stock up on supplies."

As the stable owner led the two mustangs away, Bo flicked the reins and the horse and cart moved on, past Jesse Cutler's barbershop and bath, past Doc Honeywell's surgery, until they slowed in front of Swensen's Dry Goods.

The town was swarming with women carrying baskets over their arms, and children darting out of the path of horses and carts, while men loaded supplies into the backs of their wagons. The area around Swensen's was especially busy because the Red Dog Saloon was directly across the street. Most of the ranchers who'd come to town for supplies made at least one brief stop at the Red Dog, in search of whiskey, pretty women, and Billie Conover's fine cooking.

As he brought the horse and cart to a halt Bo lifted his head and breathed in the scent of bread baking and meat roasting. "What's that?"

"I suspect Billie's already cooking up something special for supper tonight. Next to you, I'd have to say she's the best cook I've ever known."

"You don't say. It'll be nice to eat someone else's cooking for a change." With a grin he leaped down and tied his horse.

Before Kitty had a chance to step down Bo was beside her, lifting her into his arms and setting her down gently in the doorway of Swensen's. At least a dozen people stopped what they were doing to stare. Seeing them, Kitty felt her cheeks grow hot.

She shot a killing glance at a bewhiskered man standing beside the counter. "What're you looking at, Roscoe?"

At her hiss of anger, Roscoe Timmons, the bartender of the Red Dog, who was buying a pouch of tobacco, merely grinned. "Had to look twice to see if it was really you, Kitty. Don't think I've ever seen you being treated like a lady before."

"And you won't live long enough to see it again if you don't stuff that grin in your pocket."

"Sure thing." Without another word he hurried away.

"Kitty." Inga Swensen came around the counter

to greet her. "It's been a while since you were here. I was just saying to Olaf the other day that we ought to send someone out to Aaron's place and see if the two of you were all right." She glanced at Kitty's arm in the sling. "You've been hurt?"

Kitty shrugged. "Just a broken arm. Aaron wants Doc Honeywell to take a look at it while I'm in town."

"And who is this?" Inga studied the well-dressed man beside her young friend.

"Bo Chandler. Bo, this is Inga Swensen."

"Ma'am."

At Bo's greeting the pretty, white-haired woman actually blushed. "Mr. Chandler. Will you be staying long in Misery?"

"I guess that depends." He gave her one of his most charming smiles as he reached into his pocket and withdrew several envelopes. "I was hoping you might post these the next time the mail stage comes to town."

"Why, I'd be happy to, Mr. Chandler." Inga took the envelopes from his hand, aware that several of the women from town had paused in their shopping to watch and listen.

She didn't blame them. It wasn't often they had someone in Misery who was so handsome and well-spoken.

"How do you happen to be here with Kitty?"

"She saved my life."

That had heads coming up and women whispering behind their hands.

Inga glanced toward her husband, just walking in from the back of the store. "Olaf, come and meet Mr. Bo Chandler. He was just about to tell us how Kitty saved his life."

Bo could see Kitty's cheeks growing redder by the minute. She was clearly uncomfortable being the center of attention.

"Three outlaws shot me and left me for dead. If it weren't for Kitty, that's what I'd be."

"Oh, my." Inga Swensen put a hand to her throat. "How fortunate for you that our Kitty was there."

"Yes, ma'am."

Olaf Swensen elbowed his way through the crush of women who had moved closer to hear. "What is it you do, Chandler?"

"I've done a lot of things in my travels. But I'm a lawyer by profession."

"A lawyer?" Olaf exchanged a look with his wife, then caught Bo's arm. "Would you mind looking at some papers while you're here?" He lowered his voice. "I've been trying to buy some land outside of town for my son and his bride, but I'm afraid to sign the documents until I know what they say."

Bo nodded. "I'd be happy to take a look at

them.'' He turned to Kitty. ''I'll just be a minute while you're giving Inga your order.''

As he trailed Olaf Swensen toward the back room, Kitty could see every woman in the store turn and watch. She could actually hear some of them sighing.

She felt a quick flash of temper. It had to be temper. She refused to believe it could be anything as foolish, as frivolous, as jealousy. That was for the silly women who primped and wore fancy gowns and fussed over every cowboy who looked their way. It certainly wasn't for the likes of her. She'd always prided herself on having more sense than that.

Annoyed, she turned to Inga and began rattling off the list of supplies she and Aaron had agreed on.

Chapter Twelve

"I thank you, Bo." Olaf Swensen offered his hand. "I'd like to pay you something for the help you gave me."

"Instead of pay, how about some credit?" Bo accepted his handshake. "Those gunmen took off with my money and my papers. Until I contact my bank in Virginia, I'm penniless."

"It's my pleasure." Olaf indicated the shelves filled with food, clothing, grain. "Take what you need, and we'll settle up whenever you're ready."

Just as he turned away, Bo saw a tall, handsome man stride into the store and shout a greeting to Kitty. She turned, gave a little cry of delight, and flew into his arms, to be swung around and around in dizzying circles until she was giggling in a way Bo had never heard before.

He experienced a sudden, jaw-clenching flash of

jealousy that had him fisting his hands at his sides. He started forward, his eyes narrowed to slits.

Kitty took no notice as she was set none-too-gently on her feet. ''Oh, Yale. You look so good.''

''And you look as bedraggled as ever.'' He tugged on a lock of her hair. ''Now tell me how you came by this.'' He stroked a finger down the arm tied in the sling.

''I got careless around an ornery stallion.'' She turned to Bo. ''Look who's here. My brother Yale. Since he's settled down and given up his gambling ways, he's become the unofficial banker of Misery.''

''Your…brother?'' Bo found himself struggling to switch gears. A moment ago he'd been ready to throttle this man within an inch of his life. Now he found himself unclenching his fist and offering a handshake. ''Bo Chandler.''

''You the lawyer everybody's talking about?''

Bo glanced around. ''I see word spreads fast out here.''

Yale grinned. ''You'd better watch out. I know of at least half a dozen citizens of Misery who are dying for your services. In fact, if you look outside, you'll seem them starting to form a line.''

Bo looked up to see that Yale had spoken the truth. Though he never would have believed it, several men were already striding forward, holding tightly to legal-looking documents.

Within minutes the little store was swamped, with everyone shouting questions at Bo until he held up his hand for silence.

"I don't think it's fair to the Swensens that we crowd their store. Why don't we meet somewhere else, and I'll handle as many questions as I can."

"How about the Red Dog?" one of the men called. "Jack Slade won't object to a few more customers."

Bo nodded. "All right. I'll meet you there in a little while." As they began filing through the doorway he turned to Kitty. "But first we're going to see Doc Honeywell, and have him take a look at that arm."

She gave a reluctant nod of her head. "All right. After that I want to see my brother Gabe." She looped an arm through Yale's. "Want to come with us?"

"You bet." He tucked her hand in his. "Since Cara is helping Billie with the cooking at the Red Dog, I figure we can all have a midday meal there." He glanced over her head at Bo, striding along beside them. "You're in for a treat when you taste Billie's cooking."

Bo grinned. "That's why I agreed to the suggestion to meet at the Red Dog. After the way Kitty bragged, I figured I'd be a fool to miss this opportunity."

Yale winked at his little sister. "A smart man. I like that."

Kitty, walking between them, wondered at the lightness around her heart. But there was no time to ponder her feelings as she stepped into Doc Honeywell's surgery.

The old man looked up when they entered. "Yale. Kitty." He spied the sling. "What was it this time?"

"An angry mustang. I just sold him to Eli Moffat."

The doctor gave a hearty laugh as he began rolling the sleeves of his white shirt. "That'll teach him."

"Doc, this is Bo Chandler."

The two men shook hands before the doctor untied the sling and began examining the splints and dressings. After a careful examination he looked up. "Who's responsible for this?"

"I am." Bo was looking over his shoulder.

"You a doctor?"

"No, sir."

"You sure? This looks better'n anything I could do."

Bo shrugged. "I used to room with a medical student."

"Where was this?"

"When I went east to study law. A university in Boston."

At that the doctor paused in his examination and

studied the man with sudden interest. "Boston? That wouldn't be Harvard University, would it?"

"Yes, sir."

"You don't say." Deep in thought, he returned his attention to Kitty's arm. "You're lucky, young woman. That bone is mending just fine. I think you can leave off the splint and dressings now. It'll feel weak for a while. You'll have to go easy with it until you have the full strength back."

"You mean it?" Her face was wreathed with smiles. "I can go back to doing what I did before?"

Doc Honeywell gave a sigh. "You're not listening, Kitty. I don't want you leaping right back into the saddle to break mustangs just yet. Give yourself a little time."

"Huh," she sniffed. "Time."

Hearing the disgust in her tone he patted her on the shoulder and turned to Bo. "What's a smart Harvard-educated lawyer doing here in Misery?"

"Working, apparently."

When the doctor gave him a puzzled look Yale explained. "The minute word got out that we had a lawyer in town, it seemed everyone had a question for him. Near as I can tell, Bo has about two hours' worth of work waiting for him over at the Red Dog."

Doc chuckled. "I'm not surprised. You know, Bo, if you wanted, you could probably find enough business from the folks here in town and the ranchers nearby to set up a lucrative practice right here in Misery.''

As a shadow fell over them they looked up to see a tall, muscular man in the doorway. His sheriff's badge winked in the sunlight.

''Gabe.'' Kitty danced across the room and offered a much more subdued greeting to her older brother. ''Doc says I can use my arm again.''

''I didn't know you'd lost the use of it. What happened?''

''Nothing much. Just a nasty mustang stallion.'' She led him across the room. ''Gabe, this is Bo Chandler. He's the one who set my broken arm.''

''Then I'm obliged to you, Bo.'' Gabe offered his hand.

''Your sister isn't telling the half of it.'' After shaking his hand Bo added, ''She had a dislocated shoulder and a couple of broken ribs. I don't know how she made it back to Aaron's without passing out cold.''

The three men turned to Kitty, whose cheeks had gone bright pink. ''There you go again. Trying to make a fuss over me. I'm fine now, and that's all that matters.''

''Maybe.'' Gabe studied her with a critical eye. ''But I worry about you and that old man way out there in the middle of nowhere.''

"Aaron and I are just fine." She flushed under his scrutiny. "Besides, we have Bo there now."

Gabe turned to him with a steely look and spoke for both himself and Yale. "You're living out at Aaron's place?"

"That's right."

"Those are pretty cramped quarters." Yale seemed to be taking his measure. "Where're you sleeping?"

"In the barn." Bo was grateful that Aaron had intervened when he did. He had the sense that these two would be more than happy to tear him apart limb from limb if they thought he was sleeping anywhere near their little sister. He nodded toward the door. "I think I'd better get over to the Red Dog and start looking at a few legal documents."

Gabe arched a brow. "What's this all about?"

Yale inclined his head. "Come on. Join us at the Red Dog. I'll explain along the way." He turned to the doctor. "You coming, Doc?"

The old man grabbed up his coat and began unrolling his sleeves. "I wouldn't miss it."

It was quite a sight in the Red Dog. Jack Slade, after introducing himself, returned to a poker game, taking Doc Honeywell along to join in. They left Bo to conduct his business at a table near the door. While Kitty and her brothers sat at a nearby table,

catching up on family news, Bo read legal documents, answered hundreds of questions, and offered
advice on land purchases, debts, personal property,
and even, for one grizzled cowboy, the proper way
to dissolve a marriage.

When Billie and Cara emerged from the kitchen
to join their husbands, Kitty laid a hand on Bo's
shoulder and leaned close to whisper, "If you want
to taste Billie's cooking, you'd better do it now."

He stood. "Excuse me, gentlemen. I'll be back in
a little while."

As he walked away, the men still waiting to talk
to him began muttering among themselves. It was
plain, after hearing his fancy words and his ease with
legal terms, that he knew what he was talking about.

When he reached Kitty's table Bo smiled at the
two women who were busy serving platters of roast
chicken and thick slabs of home-baked bread.

"Bo, this is Billie and Cara."

He doffed his hat to the two women who looked
so different. Billie, with wild red tangles that spilled
down her back, was wearing an apron so big it was
tied around her twice. The hair at her temple was
damp with sweat from the kitchen. Cara had dark,
silky hair and a calm, quiet demeanor. Both women
greeted him warmly before taking their places beside
their husbands.

He held Kitty's chair before sitting next to her.

Yale indicated the other table. "You looked pretty busy over there."

Bo nodded. "I'm surprised at how starved everybody seems for legal answers."

Gabe studied him over the rim of his coffee cup. "The only legal advice available here in Misery is when a visiting judge comes through town. And he's usually so busy conducting trials, there's no time left for answering questions."

Bo took a bite of his food before looking up with a smile. "Kitty told me I'd be enjoying a fine meal here at the Red Dog. I just didn't expect it to be this fine."

Billie and Cara blushed with pleasure.

Gabe moved his food around his plate and cleared his throat. "You planning on staying at Aaron's place, Bo?"

The others fell silent.

Bo shrugged. "I haven't made any plans one way or the other. I guess I just figured I'd take things a day at a time."

Gabe nodded. "You could always take a room here at the Red Dog."

"No." The word was out of Kitty's mouth before she could stop it. Seeing the others staring at her she ducked her head. "I mean, Aaron enjoys Bo's company. Besides, Bo's real handy. He fixed the door and replaced the steps on the porch. He made us a new bench and repaired my chair. And he can cook.''

''Cook?'' Both women spoke at the same time.

''That's right. And you know how much Aaron and I hate to cook.'' Kitty knew she was talking too fast, but she couldn't seem to stop herself. ''And best of all, when I broke my arm, Bo stepped in and took over the training of the mustangs, so we'd have enough money for supplies.''

Through it all, Bo had gone silent, watching the reaction of Kitty's family.

''So you don't have any money of your own?'' Yale studied him with keen interest.

''Not with me. The gunmen who shot me helped themselves to my money and papers.''

''So you say.'' Yale glanced at Gabe. ''And you're living off the kindness of our sister and an old man.''

''Yale...''

Kitty started to protest, but Bo put a hand on her arm and turned to her brother. ''That's true.''

''I want you to know something, Chandler.'' Yale's tone hardened. ''My brother and I have been watching out for our little sister since we were no bigger than pups.''

Bo's eyes narrowed fractionally. ''I've seen how you've been looking out for Kitty. I've been there for weeks now, and this is the first I've laid eyes on either of you.''

''Why, you…''

Gabe started to rise, but Billie put a hand on his arm. ''Before you two head back to Aaron's ranch, stop by the kitchen. I'll have a parcel of food to take home.''

Bo gave her a quick smile. ''Thank you, ma'am. We're obliged.''

''And Kitty.'' Cara, eager to calm the anger in her husband, added softly, ''Bo's right. We have been neglecting you lately. Maybe, if you don't mind, we could ride out to the ranch next Sunday after services and have a visit with you and Aaron.''

Kitty nodded, grateful for the kindness of her two sisters-in-law. ''Aaron would really like that. The trip into town is too much for him now.'' She pushed away from the table. ''I'd better get over to Swensen's and see if Olaf has loaded our supplies in the cart.'' She sent a pleading glance toward Bo. ''Would you come along with me?''

He shook his head. ''Sorry. I still have a few more questions to answer at the other table. I'll be along in a few minutes.'' He nodded toward Gabe and Yale, then gave a last smile at their wives. ''Nice to have met all of you.''

As he strode across the room he was mobbed by men waiting to talk to him.

From their vantage point, Gabe and Yale Conover watched and listened. Then, as their wives returned to the saloon kitchen, they bent their heads close.

"What do you think?" Gabe flicked a glance toward Bo.

Yale shrugged. "If we believe Kitty, the man's a saint who can do everything. But he could just as easily be a hustler who's been drifting around the country looking for the perfect mark. It doesn't get much better than a lonely female and a helpless old man."

Gabe couldn't help chuckling. "Don't let Kitty and Aaron hear the way you've just described them."

Yale grinned. "Yeah. Or that lonely female will have my hide, and that helpless old man will help her tan it." His smile faded. "Still, he bears watching. What could possibly attract him to that miserable old shack in the middle of nowhere?"

Gabe nodded. "I've been thinking the same thing. I don't like this at all. I intend to go back to the jail and check out every Wanted poster in my desk, to see if any of the drifters and hustlers match the description of Bo Chandler."

The two brothers shoved back their chairs and shook hands, before going their separate ways.

But not before giving Bo Chandler several long, calculated looks.

Chapter Thirteen

When Kitty returned to Swensen's, Inga and the other women from town were waiting. The looks on their faces reminded her of a family of mountain cats watching their prey. The moment she stepped through the doorway they pounced.

"Where's your Mr. Chandler?" Inga glanced around expectantly.

"He's not 'my' Mr. Chandler." Kitty could feel her temper rising as she added, "He had business to conduct at the Red Dog." She nodded toward the back door, eager to escape. "Has Olaf loaded my supplies yet?"

"He's seeing to it now." Inga wasn't about to let her go so easily. "How long have you known Mr. Chandler?"

"A few weeks."

"He said you saved his life." Emma Hardwick sidled closer. "How romantic."

Kitty wrinkled her nose. "A bullet in the back isn't very romantic, Emma. Besides, how'd you hear about that?"

The young woman smiled. "He told Jesse, who told his wife, who told me."

"And you saw to it that the whole doggone town heard it from you."

Instead of being insulted, Emma merely nodded. "Indeed they did. And those who haven't heard it yet, soon will. Are we to understand that Bo Chandler is living with you and Aaron?"

Kitty could feel her hackles beginning to rise. "That's right. That's what neighbors do for neighbors. The only other place he'd be welcome to stay is at the Red Dog." She watched Emma's reaction, knowing the animosity between this righteous young woman and Jack Slade. "Maybe I ought to suggest he take a room over there."

"That den of iniquity." As expected, Emma's smile was wiped from her lips. "If you only knew the sad tales I hear from the women I've rescued from that wretched life."

Kitty turned away, determined to make good her escape. "Sorry. I don't have time right now, Emma."

She was so relieved to see Eli Moffat just entering the store she latched on to his arm like a dog with

a bone. Minutes later, he handed her the money for
the mustangs and the two exchanged handshakes.

Kitty crossed to Inga and the two women began
going over the cost of the supplies. Minutes later
they hugged and Kitty walked to her cart, loaded
with sacks of flour and sugar.

Before she could pull herself up to the seat, she
saw Bo step out of Jesse Cutler's barbershop and
bath. At the sight of him her heart did a funny little
dip. As he crossed the street she saw the way heads
turned and people stared. She was assaulted by so
many emotions, she didn't know how to sort through
them. There was, of course, a sense of pride, that he
was looking at her and smiling. But there was also
a funny little feeling of fear, that anyone watching
might mistake that smile for something more than
friendship.

He paused beside the cart, freshly shaved, his hair
neatly trimmed and dripping with beads of water.
''Just give me a minute, Kitty. I have some business
to settle at Swensen's.''

Because she couldn't seem to find her voice, she
simply nodded. When he disappeared inside the
store she found herself staring around at the dusty
little town, trying to see it through Bo's eyes. She
had nothing to compare it with, since this was the
only place she'd ever been. What did Boston look
like? San Francisco? She tried to imagine, but it was

impossible. Still, though Misery must seem small next to those big cities, she figured it had everything necessary for survival. A doctor. A lawman. A dry goods store. A barbershop and bath. What more could anyone possibly want or need?

A short time later Olaf Swensen stepped up to the cart and began loading several parcels in the back with her supplies. When he was done, he and Bo shook hands and Bo pulled himself up beside Kitty. Before he could flick the reins, Billie came rushing out the back door of the Red Dog, carrying a linen-covered tray.

"You wouldn't want to leave without your supper," she called.

Bo stepped down and took the heavy burden from her hands, storing it in the back of the cart before giving her a dazzling smile. "Thanks, Billie. We're much obliged."

She returned his smile before looking up at Kitty, holding a hand to her forehead to shield the late-afternoon sun from her eyes. "Don't forget. We'll be by on Sunday."

Kitty nodded. "I can't wait to tell Aaron. He'll be so happy to see everyone."

The two young women waved and called their goodbyes as Bo flicked the reins and the horse and cart rolled along the dusty street.

When they reached the end of town Kitty turned

for a final glimpse of Misery, before turning back to Bo. "What did you think of our town?"

"A fine place. Filled with even finer people."

"You don't think it's too small?"

He shrugged. "There's all kinds of building going on. I heard talk of plans for a sawmill. Misery strikes me as a town that's going to keep growing."

"You think it'll ever be as big as Boston or San Francisco?"

He laughed. "I hope not."

She swiveled her head. "Why do you say that?"

"Because their size was one of the reasons I kept moving on."

"Then you don't mind a small town?"

"Mind?" He tugged on a lock of her hair. "I think there's something special about small towns. Especially Misery. After all, you love it, don't you?"

She nodded, trying to ignore the curls of pleasure moving along her spine. "I do."

"Then I do, too."

For some reason she didn't care to probe too deeply, his words had her smiling with relief.

The sun had already made its arc across the sky, hovering just above the tips of the Black Hills. The horse and cart came up over a ridge and started across a meadow green with spring grass and dotted with wildflowers.

Bo pointed to a stream meandering over boulders, the banks lined with an occasional poplar. "That looks like the perfect spot for our supper."

She gave him a look of surprise. "You want to eat along the trail?"

He grinned. "The smell of all that food in the back of the cart has been tempting me for miles. Why not stop here and enjoy a picnic?"

"A…picnic? What's that?"

He turned to see a look of puzzlement on her face. "Are you telling me you've never enjoyed a picnic?"

"I don't even know what it is."

He thought a moment. "It's a carefree meal eaten outside."

"Must be something you learned in the East." She sniffed. "Here in the Dakotas, food's food. Whether we eat in our cabin, or along the trail, it's still just food."

He brought the horse to a halt and stepped down, circling the cart and reaching up for her before she could step down. Instead of setting her on her feet he swept her into his arms and carried her through the grass.

Against her temple he muttered, "I see I have my work cut out for me."

"Work?"

"I intend to try to change your mind about eating." He paused in a sunny spot beside the stream and set her down. "Don't move. I'll be right back."

When he walked away she sat perfectly still. Not because he'd ordered it, but because she couldn't have moved if she'd wanted to. The press of his lips and the deep timbre of his voice against her temple had sent heat spiraling through her, leaving her absolutely weak.

She couldn't remember a time when she'd actually enjoyed being lifted in someone's arms and carried. From her earliest days, she had no memory of being carried, except occasionally on Yale's back. Circumstances had forced her to be fiercely independent. A fact that gave her great pride. So why was it different when Bo carried her? What was it that she felt in his arms? Certainly not helpless, but rather…pampered.

Pampered. In her whole life, she had never before known the luxury of being pampered. But she felt that way with Bo. There had been that special bath, and the way he'd washed her hair. And now this.

Bo lifted the linen-covered tray from the back of the cart and carried it toward her. Placing the linen squares on the grass, he set the tray on them and breathed in the wonderful fragrance of roasted chicken and still-warm bread.

''Now this is a picnic.'' He handed her a chicken leg and a thick slice of buttered bread before settling himself beside her and helping himself to the same.

They ate in silence for several minutes, enjoying the sound of the birds in the nearby trees, and the gurgling of the water as it spilled over stones.

Kitty nibbled the chicken leg and grew thoughtful. ''The first time I tasted Billie's cooking, I found myself hoping she would come back to see us often. She was just the sweetest thing.'' She laughed. ''Of course, I never dreamed she and Gabe would be married one day. They seemed all wrong for each other.''

''In what way?''

Kitty shrugged, thinking back. ''Billie's always rushing around, doing a hundred different things. Gabe is slow and steady and deliberate. He's a straight-arrow man of the law. When they met Billie was a wanted woman.''

''Wanted for what?''

''For murder. But it turned out that the man she was supposed to have killed was still alive. He'd just wanted revenge because she wouldn't marry him.''

''That's quite a story.'' Bo leaned his back against the trunk of a tree and stretched out his long legs before turning to study her. ''How about Yale and Cara? Do they have a story, too?''

Kitty nodded. ''More than most folks, I suppose.

Yale always loved Cara, but because of his reputation as a wild man and a gambler, her father forbid him to come anywhere near his daughter. So Yale left Misery and traveled the West, drinking and gambling, and even joining up with a gang of outlaws. Cara married another man and had two sons. Then, with her husband dead, and her own life in danger, it was Yale who came to her rescue.''

''And now your brother is happily married and considered a fine, upstanding citizen of Misery.''

''It's funny, isn't it? Aaron's always saying that we'll never know what's just over the hill unless we're willing to make the climb.'' She sighed. ''I guess you've climbed a lot of hills from Boston to San Francisco.''

At his silence she glanced over. ''What's wrong?''

He was staring at her with the strangest look on his face. ''Nothing.''

''Yes, there is.'' Without thinking she put a hand on his and gently rubbed. ''Tell me what's wrong.''

He felt the quick rush of heat, the sudden tightening of his throat. ''It's nothing.''

''If nothing's wrong, why are you looking so fierce, Bo?''

He got to his feet. ''I think we should go.''

She scrambled up and caught his arm, her fingers tightening at his sudden flex of muscle. ''Not until you tell me what's wrong. Is it something I said? Something I did?''

"It's you. It's us." His voice was a growl of frustration.

He saw the way she stiffened as she pulled her hand away. He knew he'd confused her, but there was no help for it. The mere touch of her had the blood draining from his brain and fire raging through his loins.

Wanting to make amends he caught her by the shoulders. But the moment she turned toward him he forgot everything except the need. Dragging her close, he covered her mouth with his.

This was no lover's kiss. No tender nibble of mouth on mouth. The fingers gripping her shoulders were like steel, pressing through the buckskin to almost bruise her flesh. The lips moving over hers weren't so much coaxing as demanding. The sound that escaped his throat was something deep and primal, and brought an answering call from her as he drove her against the trunk of the tree and kissed her until they were both breathless.

"I think of you, Kitty. At night, when I'm trying to sleep. During the day, while I'm doing chores." He pressed his mouth to her throat and felt the way she trembled. "I try to stay busy. But nothing helps. You're always on my mind."

"I...think of you, too, Bo." She arched her neck, giving him easy access. "More than I care to."

"You do?" He lifted his head, struggling for air. There was something so raw, so wounded, in his eyes, she felt a flash of fear. She touched a hand to his mouth and was startled when he caught hold of it and pressed a kiss to the palm.

She gave a nervous laugh. "I never thought about a man before. I never knew one who could take up so much of my time. But you..." She shook her head and looked away. "I don't know what to make of you, Bo Chandler. All those big fancy words, and all the things you can do. Cook. Clean. Break mustangs. And this." She pulled her hand away. "You touch your mouth to my hand and it curls my toes."

He wanted to laugh but it came out on a hiss of breath. "It's the same for me. I've tried not to touch you. God knows I've tried." He lowered his head and took her mouth again. A slow, heart-stopping kiss that had his pulse roaring in his brain, and the need urging him to take and give until they were both sated.

It was what he wanted. All he wanted. And from the way she was responding, it was what she wanted, as well.

He lifted his mouth from hers and began to press soft, feathery kisses across her face.

"Why?" Kitty wondered how her hands had found their way around his neck.

"Why what?" He paused to look into her eyes. Eyes that were so open and honest, they took hold of his heart and squeezed until he could hardly breathe.

"Why have you tried not to kiss me? I like kissing you, Bo."

He couldn't help grinning. "I like kissing you, too, Kitty. But it can lead to other things."

"What other things?"

He gave her a long, probing look, trying to determine whether or not she was serious. "Kissing can lead to touching. And lying together."

"Oh. You mean, like mating?" She gave a dreamy sigh. "I haven't given that much thought, but I suppose it might not be too bad. Is that what you have in mind?"

"I…" He realized his jaw had dropped and forced himself to close his mouth. Her sweet honesty was like a splash of icy water. He suddenly remembered his promise to Aaron and forced himself to take a step back, breaking contact. "What I have in mind is getting you back to the ranch."

"Get back? Now? But why? I thought you enjoyed kissing me."

"I do. More than I ought to. But right now, we're heading back."

"I don't understand...."

Before she could issue a further protest, he turned away and began hastily packing up their picnic supplies and loading them into the back of the cart. Through it all she stood very still, watching him with a look of puzzlement.

"Come on." After helping her up to the seat he climbed up beside her and picked up the reins.

As they rolled toward home, he caught sight of the wounded look in her eyes. It only added another layer to his guilt.

What was he going to do about this? He wanted her. Desperately. The way a man wanted a woman. The only problem was, Kitty Conover was as innocent as a child. Hadn't Aaron said as much?

He'd given his word to Aaron that he'd do all in his power to keep her from being hurt. And, by heaven, he intended to keep that promise. Even if it tested him to the limit of his endurance.

Chapter Fourteen

"**W**ell. It's about time." As the horse and cart came to a halt beside the porch, Aaron got up from his chair, leaning heavily on his cane.

Kitty leaped down and bounded up the stairs, throwing herself into the old man's arms. At her fierce hug he held her a little away and studied her closely. "It appears you missed me, girl."

"I did."

"And you're missing something." He pointed. "The sling and dressing on your arm."

She nodded. "Doc says it's healing just fine. He says I can get back to doing my chores in a few days."

"That's good news."

"It is. And I have news you'll like." Out of the corner of her eye she saw Bo lift a sack of flour from the back of the cart and toss it easily over his shoulder before carrying it inside the cabin. She wasn't aware that her gaze followed his every movement. But Aaron noticed and felt a twinge of unease.

"What's the news?"

"Hmm? Oh." She dragged her gaze away from the ripple of muscle as Bo set the sack down. "Gabe and Billie and Yale and Cara are coming out here on Sunday."

"That's the best news you could bring me." He saw the way Kitty stared after Bo as he returned to the cart for more supplies. "Was there any other news in town?"

She shrugged, trying to appear casual. "When the townspeople found out that Bo was a lawyer, just about everybody in Misery had need of his help. He had to take a table in the Red Dog, where everyone lined up to get advice. They had him reading letters and documents by the dozens. I've never heard so many big words in my whole life." She lowered her voice. "I swear, he can read anything, Aaron. I never heard him stumble over a single word."

"Is that so?"

She nodded. "And you should have seen the way the men in town treated him with such respect." She lowered her voice. "Now the women were another matter. Clucking over him like a bunch of hens with a new rooster in the yard."

"Well, he does cut a fine figure." When she

turned to give him a look the old man cleared his throat. "I guess I'd better think about fixing something for supper."

"No need. Billie sent a tray of food from the Red Dog."

"She did?" He was smiling broadly as he turned away. "I'll set the table."

"Bo and I won't be joining you. We ate along the trail. He called it a picnic."

Aaron turned to study her face. "A picnic? Well now. Isn't that grand?"

"You've heard of that?"

The old man laughed softly. "My Agnes and I enjoyed a picnic or two in our younger days. As I recall it was a fine way to spend a Sunday afternoon, away from the prying eyes of our parents." He saw the flush on her cheeks before he stepped through the doorway. "Why don't you help Bo with the horse and cart. When you're through, you two can have some coffee while I enjoy Billie's good cooking."

Overhearing, Bo shook his head. "I can manage by myself. You go ahead inside, Kitty, and have a visit with Aaron while he eats his supper. I'll be along in a few minutes."

Kitty didn't need any coaxing. She followed Aaron through the doorway, filling him in on every detail of their day.

"I sold a mare to Jeb Simmons for a sow and some hams. I promised to pick them up at his farm tomorrow."

"A sow?" Aaron paused beside the table, while Kitty began unwrapping the tray of food. "You thinking about raising hogs now, girl?"

She flushed. "Billie got herself some hogs, and now she doesn't have to drive all the way out to Jeb's place for meat."

"True. But hogs take a heap of work. There's the food. The pens. The barn space. And then you'll have to butcher them when the time comes."

She frowned, then shrugged. "I guess I hadn't thought it through. Still, I had to get something for that mustang mare. I couldn't let Jeb Simmons get the best of the deal."

Aaron was grinning while he dug into the roast chicken and light-as-air biscuits. "I never figured you would, girl. Nobody's ever bested you in a horse swap yet. What about the other two mustangs?"

"Eli Moffat bought the stallion and the other mare. He paid me enough to cover all our supplies." She dug into the pocket of her buckskins and set several coins on the table. "I'm afraid this is all that's left."

Aaron eyed the money wearily. "Not much to show for all the pain you suffered at the hands of that stallion, girl."

She laid a hand over his. "We've still got the rest of the herd, Aaron. By the time I'm through breaking them to saddle, we'll have enough supplies to see us through next winter."

Bo stepped into the cabin, his arms laden with bundles. "I've unhitched the cart and put the horse in the barn."

Aaron nodded toward the parcels. "I see you did some shopping of your own. Kitty tells me you were busy lawyering all day. I guess that would fill your pockets."

"Some of the folks paid me. Others were willing to barter. Jesse Cutler offered me a bath and a haircut for the work I did for him. And Olaf Swensen said I could buy on credit from his place. So I picked up a few things I thought we could use." He unwrapped the first parcel, revealing a jar of honey. "Your brother Yale mentioned that you have a sweet tooth, Kitty."

She blushed clear to the tips of her ears before giving a delighted laugh. "Honey. Oh, Aaron. Look." She opened the jar and dipped a spoon inside, then sat back, licking each drop as though it were more precious than gold.

Bo filled three cups with coffee and pulled up a chair at the table. "You might want to try that on one of Billie's biscuits."

Kitty did, breaking open a biscuit and sharing with

Aaron, who was humming with pleasure as he polished off every sweet crumb.

The old man leaned back, satisfied. "Now that was worth waiting for."

"If you've had enough to eat, you might enjoy this." Bo unwrapped another parcel to reveal a bottle of whiskey. A third contained a box of cigars.

Aaron shook his head from side to side as he regarded the precious treasures. "Son, you're surely going to spoil me."

"That's my intention." Bo poured a tumbler of whiskey, and struck a match, holding it first to Aaron's cigar, then to his own. "No amount of cigars and whiskey can repay you for the hospitality you've given me."

"Well, now." Aaron drew on the cigar and watched a wreath of smoke curl toward the ceiling. "This is starting to feel like a special night." He regarded Bo across the table. "Kitty tells me you were reading letters and documents for the folks in town."

"That's right."

"Maybe you'd read something for me." Aaron got to his feet and shuffled across the room, disappearing into his bedroom and reappearing minutes later carrying a leather-bound book. He placed it in Bo's hand. "This belonged to my Agnes. She used to read it to me when we were young. Later, I used to read it just to try to keep her voice alive in my mind. But now that my eyesight is failing, I can't make out the words anymore.''

He eased himself into the chair and watched while Bo thumbed through the dog-eared pages.

He looked up in surprise. ''It's poetry.''

Aaron nodded.

Bo turned to the first poem and began to read aloud.

'''She walks in beauty, like the night of cloudless climes and starry skies, and all that's best of dark and bright meet in her aspect and her eyes.'''

Kitty was staring at him as he read the words. The honey was suddenly forgotten.

'''And on that cheek and o'er that brow so soft, so calm, yet eloquent, the smiles that win, the tints that glow but tell of days in goodness spent, a mind at peace with all below, a heart whose love is innocent.'''

He stopped and found himself drawn to Kitty's gaze fixed on him with such passion. ''That was written by an Englishman, George Gordon.''

''Who later became Lord Byron.'' Aaron glanced at the two young people and realized he was talking to himself. They were oblivious to his presence.

''Read more.'' Kitty leaned forward, her hands clasped together on the table. ''I've never heard poetry before.''

Bo adjusted the lantern and turned the page. His voice was low and deep with passion. "'She has a voice of gladness, and a smile and eloquence of beauty; and she glides into his darker musings with a mild and healing sympathy that steals away their sharpness ere he is aware.'"

He glanced over and saw Aaron's lips moving, speaking each word from memory. The old man's eyes were moist as he looked up.

"Thank you, son. That's one of my favorites." He turned to Kitty. "'Thanatopsis,' written by an American, William Cullen Bryant. My Agnes first read it to me when we were courting. Years later she read it to me while we crossed the Badlands in search of our future." He stubbed out his cigar before pushing himself away from the table and got up slowly, leaning heavily on his cane. "I believe, after that fine meal, and this most pleasant interlude, I'm ready for sleep."

He left the empty goblet on the table. As he passed Kitty's chair he closed a hand over her shoulder. "I'm glad you're home, girl." He glanced at Bo. "And you, too, son."

Then he was gone, leaving Kitty and Bo alone.

Kitty watched as his door closed. Her voice was hushed as she turned to Bo. "I've never heard anything like that."

"Poetry?"

She nodded. "It was so beautiful. I could feel each word here." She touched a hand to her heart.

"That's what the poet has in mind. Poetry is pure emotion. When the poet writes it he wants you to see and taste and touch, but most of all to feel."

"I did." She put a hand over his. "I had no idea there was anything like that. Hearing the words the way you spoke them. Oh, Bo, it made me feel like…" She shrugged. "Like laughing and crying at the same time. Like there was a light turned on somewhere inside me." She gave a long, deep sigh. "Will you read me some more?"

He could feel the heat from her touch spreading through his veins and knew he was treading on dangerous ground. After that scene at the picnic, he was still feeling raw. And he was quite certain she was far too vulnerable right now.

"We both need to get some sleep. We've put in a long day. I'll read some more to you another time." He set the book of poetry on the table before getting to his feet. "Good night, Kitty." He picked up the lantern and started out the door. "I'll see you in the morning."

"But I…" The protest died on her lips as the door closed behind him.

She stood listening to his footsteps as he crossed the porch, then descended the steps and started toward the barn.

For several minutes more she stood where he left her, before snatching up a lantern and moving woodenly toward the ladder that led to her sleeping loft. After climbing up, she sat in her nest of furs and eased off her boots. Blowing out her lantern she sat in the darkness, her arms around her drawn-up knees.

She was sick and tired of trying to figure out Bo Chandler. He was more of a mystery to her now than when they'd first met. Then she'd thought of him only as a wounded drifter. Now, though she knew much more about him, each new discovery brought more questions.

What was an educated man doing wandering around the country like a cowboy without a horse? Why would a man who had traveled from Boston to San Francisco be willing to stay more than a day in a shack in the middle of nowhere?

He was more changeable than the winds blowing down the Black Hills. Hot one minute; cold the next. Acting like he enjoyed kissing her, then turning away without a word of explanation.

This was the second time today he'd treated her this way. Earlier, after their picnic, he'd kissed her like a man starved for the taste of her.

Like a man out of control.

The thought had her shivering. She'd felt the same way. All hot and sweaty and icy cold at the same time. Her mind so muddled, she could hardly hold a single thought. Her body straining toward his in a way she never would have believed possible. Until she'd let him know how much she'd enjoyed it. The minute she'd admitted that she didn't know much about mating, he'd backed away. Had become a different man, all cool and calm after the storm.

And now it had happened again.

Was that it? Was it the fact that she didn't know what to do?

She scrambled up in the darkness. Too restless to think about sleep, she descended the ladder and began to pace in front of the dying fire.

Could it be that a man was afraid of a woman who didn't know about mating? Not that she didn't know, she thought as she turned and paced to the door and back. She'd seen enough animals to know what it was they did. It's just that it didn't look all that pleasurable. She'd never felt the urge to imitate them. Nor did she now, if truth be told. But she liked kissing Bo. Liked being held in his arms. Liked the way her body tingled when he touched her.

What she didn't like was all these feelings churning inside. In her entire life she'd never felt so confused. As though she'd lost her way in a forest, with no sunlight or stars to guide her, and no trail to show her the way out.

"Oh, Mama." The moan slipped from her lips

without warning, and she found herself on the verge of tears.

For one brief moment she thought about slipping into Aaron's room and pouring out her heart to him. He'd helped her through so many trials in her young life. When he didn't know the answer to something, he found someone in town who did. Still, though she trusted him as she trusted no one else, something held her back this time. She knew instinctively, in her woman's heart, that this wasn't something she could share with the man who'd raised her.

Billie would know, she thought. And Cara. Both of her brothers' wives were smart, sensible women. They had not only mated, but seemed happy with their decisions. But they were hours away in Misery. And she needed some answers now.

She paused in front of the glowing embers, her arms crossed over her chest, her bare foot tapping an angry rhythm on the wood floor. Suddenly her lips curved in a grim smile.

''You're not walking away from me again, Bo Chandler. You owe me an explanation. And this time I'm not leaving until I get at the truth.''

Chapter Fifteen

"Bo Chandler, you're a damned fool." Bo stomped into the barn and slammed the door so hard it rattled the rafters.

When he hung his lantern on a hook, the plow horse lifted its head and peered over at him before returning its attention to the pile of oats.

Bo stepped into the stall where his bedroll lay amid a pile of straw and kicked off his boots, sending them flying. After unbuttoning his shirt he tossed it aside and turned the air blue with a string of savage oaths.

What a mess he'd made of things. It was bad enough he'd let himself be ambushed by a gang of outlaws. At least he had an excuse for that one. He hadn't seen them until it was too late. But there was no excuse for this. He'd seen Kitty clearly enough. Had known right from the start that she wasn't like

any other woman he'd ever met. And still he'd allowed himself to get involved. Now he was in over
his head and about to drown, unless he found a way
to put some distance between himself and her as
soon as possible.

He had to get out of here. Though it tore at his
heart to consider leaving her and Aaron alone out
here, he was going to have to leave if he wanted to
survive. The visit to town had given him the perfect
solution. The people there were hungry for legal advice. He could take a room at the Red Dog and earn
enough to see to his needs.

His needs.

He leaned an arm on the rail of the stall and stared
at the flickering light of the lantern. What he needed
was Kitty. But what she needed was another matter
altogether. And it was her need that was important
here.

An innocent like Kitty deserved to be protected.
Shielded from the realities of life beyond this tiny
oasis. She and Aaron might see this as a hardscrab-
ble patch of land. Bo knew better. Compared with
the things he'd witnessed as he'd crossed this land,
they had created a little slice of heaven right here in
the Dakota Territory.

They loved each other in the purest sense. Looked
out for each other. As far as he could see, either one
of them would willingly die for the other. Theirs was

a relationship that few people managed to attain in this world. What right did he have to come along and place himself between that sweet old man and the innocent woman who'd been with him since childhood? Were his needs more important than theirs? Besides, hadn't he given his word to Aaron that he wouldn't do anything to hurt Kitty?

That promise stuck in his throat like a stone that couldn't be swallowed and couldn't be dislodged.

There was only one solution for it. He would leave in the morning. Before this passion simmering inside him threatened to take them both down.

Though he knew it was the right thing to do, the decision didn't make him feel any better. In fact, it just made things worse. He might as well start packing his saddlebags now. There'd be no sleep for him tonight.

He rolled his discarded shirt into a ball and began stuffing it into the saddlebag that hung over the top rail of the stall.

When he heard the barn door being yanked open he looked up in surprise.

Spotting Kitty standing there, his scowl deepened. "I figured you'd be sleeping by now."

"I'm too riled up to think about sleeping." She closed the door and leaned against it a moment before starting toward him. Her eyes were as dark as the sky just before a storm. "I want you to answer me something. I..." She gaped at the shirtsleeve hanging out of his saddlebag. "What are you doing?"

He followed her gaze and swore under his breath. "Packing. I thought maybe I'd go into town tomorrow."

"Why?"

He shrugged. This wasn't the way he'd planned on telling her. It would have been easier to swallow in the morning, after she and Aaron had polished off a good breakfast.

Her eyes flashed fire. "You were going to sneak off in the night, weren't you?"

"Of course not. I..."

"What else do you have in there?" She strode past him and hauled the saddlebag down, rummaging a hand inside. When she came up empty, she tossed it aside. "What is this all about, Bo? Why were you planning to sneak away?"

"I'm not sneaking. I planned to go tomorrow, after telling you and Aaron the truth."

"What is the truth?" She poked a finger in his bare chest and, too late, realized her mistake. Her entire hand was tingling from the contact with his naked flesh. She lowered her hand to her side where she clenched it into a fist.

He was fighting his own demons. The mere touch

of her had him sweating. "I told you. I intend to go to Misery tomorrow."

"Why?"

"I've accepted your hospitality long enough." He saw her reaction and hated himself for hurting her like this. But now that he'd taken this first step, there was no going back. He'd just have to muddle through.

"What if I...?" She nearly groaned at the slip of her tongue. "What if we don't want you to go?" She emphasized the *we*.

"You'll both be relieved once I'm gone." He turned away, needing to escape the wounded look in her eyes. It was ripping his heart out.

"I told you that I came out here to ask you something." When he didn't turn around she stared at the wide expanse of his shoulders, the ripple of muscle across his back and experienced a ripple of something similar deep inside. Why did the sight of his half-naked body affect her in this way?

She took a deep breath. "Do you enjoy kissing me, Bo?"

"Do I...?" He did turn then, and might have laughed except that his temper was still too close to the surface. Besides, she looked so serious.

He had nothing to lose by being perfectly honest. "As a matter of fact, I enjoy it very much."

"Then why...?" She ran a tongue over lips that

had gone suddenly dry. As had her throat. "Then why do you kiss me for a while and then stop and turn away?"

He kept his tone deliberately flat. "Because I don't think you're ready for the next step."

"You mean mating?"

A smile threatened, but he managed to contain it before nodding. "Something like that."

She lashed out, her fist punching his shoulder so hard it knocked him backward. Her flash of anger caught him by surprise.

"You mangy, flea-bitten son of a mule. What gives you the right to say what I'm ready for?"

He brought a hand to his shoulder and rubbed the tender spot. "Because you're as easy to read as Aaron's book of poetry. You don't know the first thing about men and women."

"Maybe I don't. But I can learn."

"Kitty." He reached for her but she stepped back. Annoyed, he gave a hiss of breath and lowered his hands to his sides. What was he supposed to do about this ornery, annoying female?

Her eyes were narrow slits. "I'm not stupid, Bo. Whatever I need to know, you can teach me."

He was already shaking his head. "It isn't like learning to read."

"I learned to like kissing, didn't I? And I even

learned to like having your hands on me. So why can't I learn to mate?''

"It isn't something to be learned. It's something we have to choose to do. We aren't animals. There's more to it with people. It involves the heart as much as the head. It involves the senses as well as the intellect. And some people, like some animals, mate and then move on, never to see each other again.''

Her chin came up. ''Is that what's bothering you, Bo? Are you afraid if we mate, I'll try to hold you here against your will?''

He shook his head, feeling such a welling of frustration. "I'm not afraid of anything except that you'll be hurt. I gave my word to Aaron that...''

The minute the words were out of his mouth he regretted them. But it was too late. Kitty was looking at him as if he'd struck her.

''You discussed this with Aaron? You talked about us mating?''

"Of course not. Well, not in so many words.'' His anger exploded. ''And stop calling it mating. What I'm feeling for you isn't just some damnable physical joining like two animals. It's love, damn it.''

''Why, you miserable excuse for a...'' Her mouth opened once, then closed. Whatever words she'd been about to shout were completely forgotten. As was her anger. It had drained away in a single instant.

She stared at him, her eyes huge. "You...love me?"

He turned away and gripped the top rail of the stall, wondering how in the world they had come to this. What had ever possessed him to blurt out such things?

She reached a hand to his shoulder and felt him flinch.

Flinch? At her touch?

She felt a wave of pure delight bubble up to the surface, splitting her lips in a smile. He wasn't running from her because of her ignorance. He was as afraid of these feelings as she was.

Suddenly, it was all beginning to make sense.

"You love me, Bo." This time it wasn't a question. Her voice was husky and trembling with the wonder of it. "You love me."

Annoyed, he made no reply.

"And these things I'm feeling. Hot and cold and miserable and happy whenever I'm around you." She took a deep breath. "It must be love I'm feeling, too. If it isn't, I'm coming down with some powerful sickness."

She heard a sound and thought it might be a cough. When the truth dawned, her eyes narrowed. Not a cough but a laugh. She gave him a sharp rap on the back. "Are you laughing at me, Bo Chandler?"

He turned and gave out with a rumble of laughter. "Oh, Kitty. I'm laughing at us." He dragged her into his arms and pressed his mouth to her temple. "Aren't we a pair?"

"You mean you're feeling as miserable as I am?"

"Even worse. I want you so badly my teeth ache."

"Oh, Bo." Her hands found their way around his neck, and she lifted her face to his. "Is there a way to end all this suffering?"

"You want me to break my promise to Aaron?"

She touched her mouth to his and heard his quick intake of breath. Drunk with power, she rubbed her lips over his until she felt his arms tighten around her. "I don't know anything about that. As far as I'm concerned, you and Aaron had no right trying to decide what's best for me without asking me. But be warned, Bo Chandler. I'm not leaving this barn until you teach me everything you can about men and women."

For a moment he went so still she had to tip her head back to see what was wrong. He was staring at her with a look that had her heart leaping to her throat.

She saw the muscle working in his jaw as he

clamped his mouth shut and started to shake his head in refusal.

She knew her voice was trembling, but she couldn't help it. "Don't tell me no or I'll die. I swear I will, Bo."

He tried to draw back, but she held on with the same fierce determination she used in dealing with a mustang. "Kiss me, Bo."

He thought of all the reasons why he shouldn't. But there was only one reason that mattered. He had no will left to resist. He was, after all, only a man. A man so desperately in love, he had no fight left in him.

"Oh, Kitty. Kitty. What am I going to do about you?" He drew her close and covered her mouth with his.

The kiss seemed to spin on and on, until the floor beneath their feet swayed and dipped. She melted into him and gave a purr of pleasure, which only weakened his resistance more.

"Ummm." Her little hum of pleasure sent heat straight to his loins. "I surely do like kissing you, Bo Chandler. Do it again."

His voice was rough with impatience. "If I do, I won't be able to stop."

"I won't ask you to."

"Maybe not now, Kitty. But afterward, it will be too late to go back and change things. Whatever regrets you have then, you'll have to live with them for a lifetime.''

"It's my life, Bo. I'll be the one to decide what I want.'' She deliberately ran her hands up his chest, loving the touch of his bare flesh against her palms.

She saw his eyes narrow as he regarded her. But still he held back, until she felt a quick flutter of fear. "Kiss me, Bo.''

She lifted herself on tiptoe and pressed her mouth to his.

He returned the kiss. But this time there was no tenderness in him. The arms that crushed her against him were almost bruising as he began savaging her mouth.

For the space of a heartbeat she pulled back, startled by the roughness of his kiss. Then, as he claimed her mouth again, she leaned into him, giving herself up to the moment.

His lips moved over hers, alternately draining her, then filling her, until all she could taste was him. The dark, mysterious flavor of tobacco and whiskey, and the musky, masculine flavor that was distinctly his.

This time when he lifted his head he took in several deep, calming draughts of air.

His voice, when he finally spoke, was rougher than she'd ever heard. "If you stay here, Kitty, there'll be no going back.''

She shook her head and stared into his eyes, shocked by the passion she could read in those dark depths. "I'm not leaving. You can't force me to go."

He knew she spoke the truth. He didn't have the will to send her away. They'd already crossed a line.

He framed her face with his hands. "Then you're a fool. And I'm an even bigger one."

Chapter Sixteen

With his hands still framing her face he pressed soft butterfly kisses across her forehead, over her eyelids, to the tip of her nose.

She stood perfectly still, savoring each press of his lips, the warmth of his breath as it whispered over her cheeks.

When he paused, her lids fluttered, then opened, and she felt the jolt go straight to her heart at the way he was watching her. Not as a predator watching its prey. Not even the way some cowboys might cast an admiring glance at a passing female. He was looking at her the way a man might look at a woman he desired. It was a completely alien feeling for a woman who had never given a thought to how she looked. A woman who had spent most of her life alone, with only the creatures of the wild for company.

She could see herself reflected in his eyes, and she suddenly felt like the most loved, the most cherished woman on earth.

"That's nice. I liked kissing you, Bo." She gave him a timid smile. "I suppose we're going to make love now?"

"Soon." He couldn't help grinning. "But not just yet."

She brightened. "There's more?"

"Oh, Kitty. So much more." He drew her closer and kissed her full on the mouth, drawing out the kiss until she sighed and her lips parted. His tongue found hers and touched lightly, then withdrew. Tentatively she touched her tongue to his and gave a sigh of pleasure when he took the kiss deeper.

When he finally lifted his head she felt bereft. Seeing the questioning look in her eyes he chuckled low and deep in his throat. "Don't worry. We're not through yet. Sometimes we just need to take a moment to breathe."

"Oh." She took in a gulp of air before lifting her face to his.

That had laughter rumbling in his chest. "Kitty, you're so sweet. So dear." He traced the curve of her ear with his tongue before darting it inside.

She gasped and pulled a little away. "That tickles."

"Really? It does something else to me."

She lifted her head. "What does it do?"

His tone roughened. "It makes me want to devour you."

The way he said it made her shiver.

He dragged her close and ran soft, nibbling kisses down her throat. When he buried his lips in the sensitive hollow of her neck she gave a sigh of pure pleasure, and wondered at the strange new feelings that were assaulting her. Her heart was pounding in her chest. Her skin felt too tight. And there was a little pulse beating somewhere deep inside.

Suddenly his mouth closed around her breast. Despite the buckskin barrier, her nipple hardened, sending an odd liquid warmth spreading through her veins.

"Bo." She brought her fists to his chest to hold him at bay. Her breath was coming hard and fast. "What are you doing?"

"Pleasuring you, Kitty. And myself."

"It surely pleasures me. It…pleasures you, too?"

"Oh, yes." He rubbed his lips over hers. "Everything about you pleasures me."

"All right, then."

At her willingness to please he couldn't help smiling.

"This is in the way." He brought his hands to the hem of the buckskin shirt. "I need to see you, Kitty.

All of you.'' He slipped the shirt over her head, then tugged the buckskin leggings aside.

His gaze burned over her, and at the look in his eyes, her heart raced like a herd of stampeding mustangs.

"Oh, Kitty. Who would have ever believed you hid such a beautiful body under those rough clothes?''

And she was beautiful. Lithe and slender, like a willow, yet soft and rounded in all the right places, with high, firm breasts and a waist so slender his two hands could easily span it.

"I never gave much thought to my body." But she did now. Seeing the way he was looking at her, she felt the most curious jolt of pride, mixed with delight.

At any other time the thought of standing naked before a man would have horrified her. But with Bo it seemed the most natural thing in the world.

When he gathered her into his arms and began kissing her, she returned his kisses with a fervor that surprised her even more. She'd admitted to enjoying his kisses. But this was much more than simple enjoyment. With every touch of his lips, she felt herself growing more and more aroused.

She wanted to touch him as he was touching her. And did. Boldly. As her fingertips moved over his back, she felt again the ripple of muscles and thrilled to it.

Bo could feel the need for her growing, and struggled to bank the fire raging through his veins. He wanted her. Desperately. Craved what only she could give. But he was determined to make this, her first time, as special as possible. And so he bit down on the passion threatening to send him over the edge, and forced himself to go slowly. To touch and taste and savor her, inch by glorious inch.

Tossing aside the last of his clothes he caught her hands and lowered her to his bedroll in the hay.

Kneeling, she faced him, her eyes steady on his. "Is this when we mate?"

He shook his head. "Not yet."

"You're going to kiss me some more?"

He nodded. "If you want."

"Oh, yes. I do want."

He couldn't help laughing as he framed her face and kissed her with a sort of reverence that had her sighing. She slid her arms around his waist and held on, feeling the hay beneath them shift. Or was it the whole world turning and shifting with each kiss they shared?

The plow horse whinnied in the next stall, but neither of them took any notice. Outside, the wind sighed in the trees, and a night bird called. They never heard a sound. The flickering light of the lan-

tern made shifting patterns on the walls of the barn.
They saw only each other.

Time seemed to stand still. There were no chores
to see to. No herd to tame. No earth to plow. Now,
as darkness covered the land, and the world slept,
they had all the time in the world to learn each
other's secrets.

"Kitty. You're so special to me." He laid her
down on the bedroll and kissed her long and slow
and deep, the words whispered inside her mouth.
"So beautiful. So amazing. Kitty. My beautiful,
wonderful Kitty."

She heard him whisper her name like a prayer,
and thought it the most beautiful sound she'd ever
heard. She lay in his arms, steeped in the most exquisite pleasure. With each touch of his mouth to
hers, the pleasure grew. When he ran soft, moist
kisses across her shoulder, down her throat, she
sighed and arched, giving him easier access.

But when he closed his mouth around one erect
nipple, she was stunned by the feelings that seemed
to shoot straight to her core.

"Bo. Wait." She put a hand to his chest.

"You want me to stop?"

"Yes. No." She sucked in a breath. "It's just that
my mind gets all fuzzy. I can't think when you do
that."

"You don't need to think, Kitty." He ran openmouthed kisses across her collarbone, before slowly skimming her throat. "Just go with your feelings."

"I feel as though I'm so light I could float."

He chuckled. "Then we'll float together."

He forced himself to keep his touches light, his kisses gentle, until she once again relaxed in his arms. This time, when he brought his mouth and hands to her breasts, she didn't push away, but rather arched her body, increasing the pleasure, feeling the sensations grow and tighten until they threatened to snap her bones.

Now the look in her eyes no longer reflected fear but arousal. Seeing it he took her on a wild, dizzying ride that left her dazed and breathless.

She'd never known anything like this hard, driving need that had her body shuddering, her breath burning her lungs. Her skin felt too hot, as though at any minute she would turn into a blazing torch. She felt fluid and boneless, unable to do more than ride this river of passion.

"Bo. Please." She clutched at his waist and strained toward him.

He resisted the urge to take her hard and fast. It was what he wanted. What they both wanted. But he was determined to draw out each moment of pleasure for as long as he could. And so he feasted on her body, taking them both to the very edge of endurance.

She quivered as he moved over her, taking her to places she'd never even dreamed of. Giving her pleasure that bordered on pain. Now there was only Bo. His voice, low and urgent, as he whispered her name. The feel of those big, soft hands moving over her flesh, touching her as no man ever had. And that clever mouth, those flashing teeth, that amazing tongue, driving her ever higher.

Bo could feel his last thread of control beginning to slip away. Desire, all-consuming, was a caged beast struggling to break free. He could feel himself standing on the very edge of a precipice. One tiny step and he would find himself hurtling through space, unable to stop. Still, he had to try, for Kitty's sake. He was determined that she would experience everything he had to give her.

Hungry for more, she arched her body up to his, drawing him in. When she felt him hold back she lifted a hand to his cheek. "What is it, Bo? What's wrong?"

"You've never been with a man before, Kitty. I'm trying so hard not to hurt you."

"Hurt me? Oh, Bo. You could never do that." With a need that matched his she wrapped herself around him, drawing him deeper into that velvet warmth.

And then it was too late. He was a starving man,

and she was a banquet of delights. He had no choice but to taste, to feast.

As he entered her fully he began to move, to climb toward a distant peak.

Kitty's strength was equal to his as she moved with him, climbed with him. Her breathing grew ragged, her heartbeat thunderous. Heat clogged her lungs and sweat pearled her flesh.

The pleasure became so intense, she heard his name torn from her lips in a hoarse cry. She kept her eyes steady on his as she reached the very top of the mountain and, trembling, stepped over the edge.

She felt herself soaring until, lost among the stars, she shattered into millions of glittering fragments before drifting slowly to earth.

It was the most incredible journey of her life.

They lay, wrapped around each other, their bodies still joined, waiting for the world to settle.

Bo lifted his face from Kitty's hair and pressed his lips to her cheek. "Are you all right?"

She gave a barely perceptible nod of her head.

Alarmed, he levered himself on his hands to study her face. "What was I thinking? God in heaven, Kitty. I didn't mean to hurt you."

"Bo." Even that single word was an effort. She lifted a hand to his cheek and stroked. Her face relaxed into a dreamy smile. "I'm not hurt. I...can't describe how I feel. It was..." Her smile grew. "Amazing. Is it always like that?"

Relief poured through him. He felt his heart begin to beat again. Rolling to one side he drew her into the circle of his arms. "It can be. As long as you're with someone who matters."

She pressed a hand over his heart. "You matter to me, Bo."

"I'm glad." He closed a hand over hers. "Because you matter a great deal to me, Kitty."

"Did I...?" She felt suddenly shy. "Did I do it right?"

A grin touched the corners of his mouth. "You're a natural at it."

"I am?" Her smile bloomed. She snuggled closer, loving the feel of his body against hers.

He lifted a hand to a tangle of her hair, watching as it sifted through his fingers. "This was the first thing I saw when I opened my eyes out there in the Badlands after being shot. All these glorious golden curls looking more dazzling than the sunlight. I thought I was surely dead and that you were an angel come to tend me. And then I caught sight of your face, and it took my breath away."

"I think that was the gunshot wound," she said dryly. "It tends to make breathing painful."

He shook his head. "It wasn't the pain that robbed

me of breath. It was you, Kitty. In fact, the sight of you was the only thing that eased my pain in those first few hours.'' He leaned closer to brush a kiss over her arched brow. ''I'd never before seen an angel in buckskins.''

She couldn't help giggling. Especially when he brought his mouth to her ear to whisper, ''And all I could think of was how to get her out of those clothes and into my bedroll.''

''It's a good thing I didn't know what you were thinking or I'd have left you there to tend to yourself.''

He shot her a wicked smile. ''Just think of all the pleasure you'd have missed.''

''That's true.'' She sat up, facing him, her hair spilling around her shoulders in a wild tangle of curls. ''I suppose you'll want me to leave now and go back to the cabin.''

''Why would you think that?''

She shrugged. ''I figure you'll want to get some sleep.''

''I'm not tired. Are you?''

She shook her head, sending the golden curls dancing.

''Good. Then maybe you'd like to learn a few more things about...mating.''

Her mouth pursed into a pout as she stared down at him. ''I thought you said it wasn't called that.''

"It's called a lot of things, Kitty. But I prefer to call it loving." He leaned up on his elbows and pressed a kiss to her mouth.

She drew back. "What was that for?"

"For no other reason than I love the way you do that pouting thing with your lips. They just beg to be kissed."

She gave a devilish smile. "Then you won't object if I kiss you back?"

He folded his hands beneath his head, looking extremely pleased with himself. "Not at all." As she bent forward he added, "Of course, I won't be responsible if you get me all heated up and we have to...mate again."

She hesitated, her hands on his chest. "We can do it again?"

He felt the curl of pleasure at her touch. "Did you think that once was all we got?"

"I guess I figured if we got any more than that, we'd die from the pure pleasure of it."

His laughter rumbled up as he wrapped his arms around her and drew her down for a long, slow kiss. "Let's just test your theory. And if we have to die, I can't think of a better way to go."

The kiss deepened. And then there was no need for words as they lost themselves in the wonder of their newly discovered love.

Chapter Seventeen

Kitty awoke and lay perfectly still, absorbing so many strange, new feelings. She had never before fallen asleep in someone's arms. Had never awakened to the sound of a strong, steady beat of another's heart against her ear. And yet, with Bo, it felt so natural. So right.

With her eyes closed she listened to the familiar sounds. In the next stall the plow horse stomped a hoof and swished its tail. Outside the birds were just beginning to greet the dawn with a chorus of song. Raindrops beat a tattoo on the roof of the barn.

She opened her eyes and found Bo staring at her in that deep intense way she'd come to recognize.

''Good morning.'' He brushed his mouth over hers.

She felt the quick jolt to her heart. ''I can't believe I fell asleep again.''

"You needed it." He grinned. "I'm afraid I didn't give you nearly enough time to sleep all night."

"I'm not complaining." She lifted a hand to his cheek and felt the rough stubble of his beard. The touch of a man's face when he awoke was one more thing she'd never shared before. The thought of it made her smile.

He drew her closer to his chest, cushioning her against the straw beneath them. "Are you comfortable?"

"Umm. Yes." It was true. Though bits of straw poked through the blankets, she wasn't aware of any discomfort. She'd spent a lifetime sleeping in straw, or on grass, and even on hard-packed earth while trailing a herd of mustangs. What she found most amazing was that she and Bo had spent the entire night together in this confining space, and yet neither of them seemed eager to leave it.

She had feared that after a quick mating, Bo would send her back to the cabin. Instead they had spent the night loving, laughing, whispering. She had never before had the chance to talk to someone else about herself and her brothers. About their dangerous trek across the Badlands in search of their father. About the life she'd made for herself here with Aaron Smiler. And though it seemed strange at first, she found that she loved sharing her family history with Bo. He had a way of watching and listening with a quiet intensity that so intrigued her. Of asking questions that made her probe her own memories, taking her back in time, all the way to her grandfather's farm when she was just a toddler.

She snuggled close and played with the hair on his chest. "I loved our night together."

"So did I."

She glanced up almost shyly. "Can we do it again tonight?"

He threw back his head and laughed. "I think I've created an insatiable creature."

Her eyes widened. "What's...insatiable?"

He smiled down at her. "A hunger that's never satisfied."

"Oh." She shook her head. "You're so smart. You know so much more than I do."

"I don't know more. I just know different things than you do. But think about the things you know that I don't."

"Like what?"

He twirled a strand of her hair around his finger. "You know the hills around here the way I know words in a book. But I could never track a herd of mustangs for a hundred miles or more, without getting lost."

She thought about that a minute and smiled. "So we're both smart in different ways."

"That's right."

"And now I know what insatiable means."

He could see the way she turned the meaning over in her mind before saying, "I guess it is like hunger. We eat a fine big meal and think we'll never want food again. Then hours later we're back to thinking about something to eat."

"Exactly."

It had been that way for them all through the night. And each time, to her amazement, it was different. At times their loving had been as sweet, as easy, as if they'd done this for a lifetime. Bo had treated her as gently as if she'd been some fragile piece of glass, and he was afraid she would break. With exquisite tenderness he had stroked and petted and teased. At other times he'd revealed a dark side of himself as he'd erupted like a wild summer storm, all flash and fury and thunder. At such times he'd taken her with him into a dark chasm of raw emotions, churning, tumbling, until, spent, they lay in each other's arms and dozed for a while, until the need roused them to take each other again.

"Speaking of hunger..." He tipped up her lips and gave her one of those slow, lazy kisses that had her mind spinning and her body humming. "I'm thinking it's time." He spoke the words inside her mouth.

"For breakfast?" She tasted the warmth of his breath and felt her heart give a quick little hitch.

"I had something else in mind."

At that her eyes snapped open. She saw the way his mouth curved into a knowing smile. She wrapped her arms around his waist and buried her lips against his throat. "I like the way you think, Bo Chandler."

At the words spoken against his flesh he sucked in a breath and absorbed a series of tremors. Would it always be this way? he wondered. Would this little female always have the power to wipe his mind clear of all thought?

He'd worry about it another time. For now, it was enough to know that she aroused him as no woman ever had.

They came together in a storm of desire. With sighs and moans and whispered words they once again slipped into that sensual world known only to lovers.

Kitty lay in the bedroll and watched as Bo washed himself in a basin and began to shave. With each stroke of his blade she found her palms itching to touch his face. She loved the look of him. Those dark, piercing eyes. That high, smooth forehead. The way those lips curved into the most roguish smile. He had none of the rough edges of the cowboys who had grown up in the Badlands. Despite the fact that his hands had become calloused from ranch chores, he had the look of a gentleman about him.

When he wiped the last of the soap from his face their eyes met in the chipped mirror. The look he gave her had her heart doing a strange dance in her chest.

As he drew on his shirt she glanced at the saddlebags and was reminded of their scene the night before.

"Are you sorry I stopped you from going to Misery?"

He crossed the stall and knelt beside her. "I planned on going in order to avoid doing exactly what we ended up doing last night. But the minute you walked in here, I knew it was too late to run."

Alarmed, she sat up, ignoring her nakedness. "So, you are sorry?"

When he smiled she felt the warmth all the way to her toes. "How could I be sorry for what we shared? The only thing I regret is that I couldn't keep my promise to Aaron." He allowed his gaze to move slowly over her. "Speaking of Aaron, don't you think you ought to be getting dressed?"

"I guess so." She tossed aside the blankets and slipped quickly into her buckskin leggings and shirt. Then she glanced down at her bare feet. "I was in such a hurry last night, I left my boots up in my sleeping loft."

Bo scooped her into his arms and brushed a quick

kiss over her lips. "Good. That gives me the perfect excuse to carry you."

Kitty wrapped her arms around his neck, loving the way she felt in his arms.

As he stepped out of the barn and started toward the cabin, they caught sight of Aaron standing on the porch. Even from this distance they could see that his face was as dark as a thundercloud.

Bo pressed his lips to her temple to whisper, "Brace yourself, Kitty. We're about to walk into the eye of a storm."

As if to shield her, he tightened his grasp on her as he climbed the steps. Even when he paused beside Aaron he didn't bother to set her on her feet, but continued holding her in his arms.

"Something wrong, girl, that you can't walk?"

"She left her boots up in the loft."

Aaron ignored Bo and stared holes through Kitty. "That shouldn't affect her voice. Or did you leave that in the loft, too?"

"I can speak." She turned to Bo. "Put me down."

He did as she asked, then stood directly beside her, his hand on her shoulder. The meaning wasn't lost on Aaron. He could feel the wall going up between himself and them.

Kitty's voice didn't waver. "I've never lied to

you, Aaron, and I'm not going to start now. I want you to know. I spent the night in the barn with Bo.''

Aaron's blackbird eyes were bright with fury. ''Bo gave me his word…''

''I know about the low-down, dirty rotten promise.'' Kitty cut him off. ''You had no right, Aaron.''

''No right? Don't you think I care what happens to you, girl?''

''Of course you do. The same way I care about what happens to you. But this…'' She shook her head, wishing she knew all the fine words that Bo had at his disposal. ''…this was what I wanted. What we both wanted.''

''And what I wanted was to see that your heart didn't get broken, girl.''

''It's my heart, Aaron. You can't control that with a promise.''

''And you'd respect a man who couldn't keep his word?''

''I know about his word. I thought mine was more important.'' She shrugged. ''I can't help what I'm feeling.''

The old man turned on Bo with a snarl. ''And what are you feeling? Smug? Pleased with yourself?''

''No, sir. I'm sorry about not keeping my promise to you. There's no excuse for it. It just happened. Without any rhyme or reason. But I…''

"In my day a man asked for a woman's hand in marriage before taking her to his bed." He shot Kitty a withering look. "Go on inside and fetch your boots, girl. Bo and I have some things to say to each other."

Kitty's chin came up. "The two of you aren't going to make any more decisions about me behind my back. I'm staying."

Aaron took a deep breath, fighting to hold on to his last thread of patience. When he finally spoke his voice was calmer. "This isn't about you. It's man talk. Go now, Kitty."

She glanced at Bo, who gave a quick nod of his head.

Annoyed, she swiped an errant curl out of her eyes and stormed away into the cabin.

When the door closed behind her Aaron turned to Bo. "Walk with me to the corral."

The two men crossed the yard in silence. When they reached the corral Aaron leaned heavily on his cane as he regarded Bo with a steely look. "Whose idea was it that Kitty come to the barn?"

"It doesn't matter."

Aaron arched a brow. Some men, he knew, would offer excuses. This man offered nothing. Not a word in his own defense.

The old man cleared his throat. "I suspect it was Kitty's idea. She's always been headstrong."

Bo held his silence.

"I suppose you put up a good fight, but she finally wore you down?"

Bo's lips thinned and he turned to look at the mustangs milling about in the corral. Just thinking about the storm of passion Kitty had unleashed in him had his blood heating. But there was no way he could explain to Aaron, without causing further pain to the old man.

The spring breeze ruffled Aaron's white hair. Watching Bo, a slow smile spread across his mouth. "Now that I think of it, Agnes did much the same to me."

Bo's head swiveled. He regarded Aaron with a look of surprise.

"I saw the way Kitty was looking at you last night when you were reading the verses from my book. I have to say it scared me something fierce. I remember that same look in my Agnes's eyes the night she came to me. I was so determined to do the right thing. But son, there's nothing like a woman's heart to turn even the strongest man's will to jelly."

"You're not...disappointed in us?"

Aaron gave a grunt. "I guess I was, until I saw the way Kitty was so quick to defend you. Then I realized that some things never change through the ages. And this powerful drive between men and women is one of them." He paused a moment before adding, "I love her more than life, son. If you hurt her, I'll do whatever I can to make you sorry."

"I understand. And I give you my word, Aaron, I'll do everything in my power to see that she's never hurt."

"I guess that's all a man can ask." Bo offered his handshake and Aaron accepted.

Minutes later when they entered the cabin Kitty hurried over to stand between them, looking from one to the other for signs of a fight. Seeing none, she shot Bo a puzzled glance.

Instead of reassuring her, he merely touched a hand to her cheek before turning away to put the blackened kettle over the fire. Then he started breaking eggs into a pan.

To end the uncomfortable silence Kitty said, "I think after breakfast I'll pick the next mustang to break to rope and saddle."

"You feeling up to that, girl?" Aaron picked up a knife and started slicing bread.

"I won't try to ride yet. But I can lasso one of the mares and start leading her around the corral. Get her used to my scent and voice."

Aaron nodded. "I know you've been anxious to get back to them." He lifted the kettle and filled three cups with steaming coffee. "How about you, Bo? What've you got planned for the day?"

Bo shrugged. "I think after breakfast I'll head into

Misery. That is, if you'll give me the loan of one of your horses.''

Kitty turned on Aaron. ''You ordered him out of our home?''

Aaron seemed as surprised as Kitty. ''I did no such thing.'' He turned to Bo. ''Why are you going to town, son?''

Bo flipped the eggs onto three plates. As he set them on the table he gave them both a smile ''I was surprised to learn how many folks in Misery are in need of a good lawyer.''

''But…''

Before Kitty could finish he held up a hand. ''I can't keep on accepting your hospitality forever, without giving something back.''

Kitty was already shaking her head. ''But you've already given us so much. You cook and clean. You tamed the stallion and two mares. You've mended more things around here in the past few weeks than I was able to mend in a year.''

''That isn't enough. My true calling is as a lawyer. And the only place I can use that knowledge is in Misery.''

Kitty's voice turned pleading. ''But it takes hours to ride there and back.''

He nodded. ''I'll need to give that some thought. I suppose if I have to, I'll spend an occasional night at the Red Dog.'' Seeing Kitty's frown he added,

"I'm thinking I might be able to rent some space in the back room of Swensen's to meet with people in need of my help. Just until I can find something else."

Kitty's eyes were as stormy as Aaron's had been a short time earlier. "Why are you doing this now, Bo?"

Aware that Aaron was watching, he merely laid a hand over hers and gave her a gentle smile. "I figure it's time I started earning some money and thinking about the future."

The future.

At those words, whatever protest she'd been about to offer died on her lips. Her heart stuttered once, twice, before doing a wild dance inside her chest.

She wouldn't think about the time he would have to spend away from her. Instead she would concentrate on the reason for this latest sacrifice.

He was thinking about the future. Did that mean a future with her?

She knew instinctively that she would do any chore, pay any price, to guarantee a future with this man, who already owned her heart completely.

"Afternoon, Bo." Jack Slade stood outside the swinging doors of the Red Dog, holding a match to the tip of a fine cigar. "I heard you were in town. Care for a drink?"

Bo paused, shaking his head. "Sorry. No time. But I appreciate the offer."

"Where're you off to?"

"Olaf Swensen wants me to look at a room he has available in the back of his store. Just until I can find something more permanent."

"What's wrong with using a table in my place?"

Bo smiled. "There's nothing wrong with it. And I'm grateful for the use of it. But there are some folks in town who aren't comfortable with meeting a lawyer in a saloon."

"You mean like...?" Slade's eyes narrowed when he caught sight of Emma Hardwick heading straight toward them. She was wearing a dress of apple green, buttoned clear to her throat, and perched on her head was a silly bonnet in a matching shade of green. One little curl had worked its way loose of the bun at her nape, and dipped flirtatiously over her brow.

He swore under his breath and braced himself for her latest assault on his character.

Instead, she merely looked through him and smiled at the man beside him. "Mr. Chandler. You're just the one I was hoping to see. I wonder if we could talk."

Bo nodded. "I was just heading over to Swensen's. Would you like to walk along?"

"Thank you." She turned her back on Jack Slade

and placed a hand on Bo's arm as she stepped into the street.

Slade drew in a quick breath and caught the lingering fragrance of lilac water. His eyes narrowed on the sway of her hips. Damned frigid old maid. Always making him feel like dirt because he ran a saloon.

He glanced through the swinging doors and caught sight of one of his women, wearing a low-cut gown that revealed more than it covered, draping herself around a trail-weary cowboy. The sight of her didn't stir him half as much as the sight of the female just stepping into Swensen's beside Bo Chandler.

He lifted the cigar to his mouth. But it couldn't erase the scent of prim Emma Hardwick. What was he to do about her? Lately he'd actually begun to think he could turn the Red Dog into a fine hotel. With Emma as his partner.

The thought had him frowning as he turned away. He must be losing his mind.

In Swensen's, Bo shook hands with Olaf and Inga, then settled himself behind the scarred wooden table he would use for a desk. After listening to Emma Hardwick's complaints about the Red Dog, and advising her that there was nothing she could legally do to stop Jack Slade from operating a business that permitted drinking and gambling, he began to deal with the dozen or more people who waited patiently for their turn.

Jesse Cutler wanted to sue Buck Reedy for showing up drunk in his barbershop and making a mess on the floor.

Doc Honeywell wanted to know if there was any way to collect for a surgery he'd performed on an outlaw who had later gone to prison.

Jeb Simmons was buying more land, and wanted Bo to read the contracts to him. Bo found himself laughing after Simmons left. Kitty had been right. The hog rancher would probably own half the Dakotas before long.

Kitty.

He got to his feet and started out the door. It was time to get started for home if he wanted to make it before dark.

Home. He was grinning as he waved to Inga and Olaf and pulled himself into the saddle. Who would have ever believed he could think of this simple little dot on the map as home?

But it wasn't the town he was thinking of. It was the woman who had taken over his heart. He couldn't wait to hold her. To lie with her. To love her all through the night.

Chapter Eighteen

"Girl." Aaron got up from his chair on the porch and called to Kitty, who was circling the corral with one of the mustangs in tow. "Look who's coming."

Seeing the wagon bearing her family, Kitty untied the rope and let herself out of the corral. By the time she was standing beside Aaron, the wagon had rolled to a stop and Gabe and Yale stepped down. From the back of the wagon came squeals of pleasure as Billie and Cara climbed out, followed by Cara's two sons.

As they hugged in greeting, Bo ambled up from the barn where he'd been mending a stall.

"I hope you're all feeling hungry," Billie called as she began lifting assorted pots and linen-wrapped parcels from the back of the wagon. "Cara and I were up at dawn baking egg custard."

"My favorite." Aaron touched a hand to his heart.

"And I made mashed potatoes and turnips," Cara added with a smile.

Aaron arched a brow. "Does that mean I have to eat some of that before you'll let me have the custard?"

"Oh, you." Cara dimpled, then turned to Bo. "Everybody in Misery's been talking about you and the fact that you're spending so much time there now."

He grimaced. He had the sore backside to prove it. He spent hours in the saddle, dividing his time between the ranch and the town. Though it would have been simpler taking a room at the Red Dog, he couldn't bear the thought of being away from Kitty for even one night. Their nights spent in his bedroll had become his reward for all the hours of hard work. Now that he'd unlocked the secrets of her heart, she was proving to be as untamed in his arms as she'd been on the trail of her mustangs.

Cara dropped an arm around two boys. "I don't believe you've met my sons, Bo. This is six-year-old Seth and eight-year-old Cody."

Bo offered a handshake and the little boys studied him with interest.

It was Cody who spoke first. "I heard Tim Cutler telling Minnie Simmons that you're a lawyer."

"That's right."

"He says you can read anything, even words nobody's ever heard of before. Is that true?"

Bo grinned. "Well, the law likes to use big words. Personally I'd rather use words the average rancher can understand."

"But how'd you learn to read like that?"

Bo knelt down, until he was eye level with the boy. "I was lucky enough to have a father who was also a lawyer. He was my first teacher. Later I went away to school."

"We don't have to go away to learn. We've got a school in Misery." Seth, not to be outdone by his older brother, stepped up beside him. "Miss Hardwick teaches us reading and writing two days a week now."

"That's good." Bo gave the boy an encouraging smile. "Can you read, Seth?"

"Yes, sir. Well," the boy admitted shyly, "some. But only little words."

"That's all right. The little words will grow into bigger ones. And before you know it, you'll be reading more and more words until even the biggest ones won't stump you."

"Is that how it was with you?" the boy asked.

Bo nodded before getting to his feet. Seeing the women carrying their food up the steps he gallantly hurried ahead to hold the door for them.

As she stepped through the doorway Billie breathed deeply. "Something smells wonderful."

Bo nodded toward the fireplace, where a side of deer roasted over a spit. "I've been roasting that venison all day, in anticipation of your arrival." Glancing out the window he added, "Kitty and Aaron have been as excited about your visit as two kids at Christmas."

Billie shared a look with Cara before saying, "We both feel a little guilty. It's so easy to get caught up in our own lives and forget about Aaron and Kitty way out here."

"They understand. And their own lives are busy and satisfying. But I know family means a lot to Kitty. As for Aaron, those three are all he has left."

The two women nodded their agreement before bustling about the kitchen, preparing the food they'd brought.

Outside the boys chased each other in a game of tag while the men trailed Kitty to the corral, where they leaned on the rails and studied her latest herd of mustangs.

"How many more do you have to break to saddle?" Gabe asked.

"Eight. I gave a dappled mare to Bo, to use for his trips to Misery. The sooner I get the rest of these tamed, the sooner I can buy more seed. With all the interruptions this spring, I'm late getting the crops planted.''

Yale hooked a thumb toward the cabin. "What's the matter with your new boarder? Is he too busy with his fancy book learning to help you plow?''

Kitty's eyes blazed. "That's not fair, Yale. Bo's done plenty of chores around this place.''

"So you say.''

At Yale's tone of sarcasm she said, "He's mended the steps. Straightened the door. Repaired a broken window. Just today he nailed up planks for a new stall. There isn't anything around here Bo can't do.'' She turned to Aaron. "Isn't that right?''

The old man nodded. "I don't know what we'd do without Bo around to lend a hand.'' He leaned on his cane and studied the two brothers, who wore identical frowns. "I think there's something you aren't saying. What's this all about?''

Gabe and Yale exchanged a look.

Gabe shrugged. "Nothing we can say for certain. It's just a feeling we have.''

Kitty's hands fisted on her hips. "And just what is this feeling?''

"That he might be a slick drifter, who isn't above using his charms to take advantage of the two of you.''

For a moment Kitty was too stunned to say a word

in Bo's defense. Beside her, Aaron had gone very still.

He turned to Gabe. "You say it's just a feeling. I take it there's a whole lot more to this than you've told us."

Yale looked uncomfortable. "As you know, I'm the unofficial banker in Misery. So when a stranger came to town and asked Olaf Swensen where he could take a bank draught for cashing, Olaf sent him to me. I told the stranger he'd have to send a letter to his bank back home asking for approval before I could give him any money. I helped him with the letter and offered to send it on the next stage." He glanced at Gabe before adding, "The man said his name was Beauregard Chandler."

Kitty clapped a hand to her mouth.

Aaron's eyes narrowed. "Are you thinking Bo has assumed another man's identity?"

The two brothers remained silent.

Aaron turned to Gabe. "Have you had any Wanted posters for someone who answers Bo's description?"

Gabe shook his head. "Not yet. But I'm keeping my eye out. Yale and I both think it's odd that a man with as much schooling as Bo Chandler claims he has, would be willing to settle in a dusty little place like Misery. Why would he live way out here, so far from town, unless he was hiding from something? And what about this man who claims the same name? Which of them is telling the truth, and which one is the liar?''

Kitty felt a jolt, and was reminded that she'd had similar questions of her own. But that was before. Before she'd been won over by Bo's charm. Before she'd completely lost her heart. Before she'd opened to him, sharing not only her body, but her innermost thoughts and dreams, as well.

Still, she could see by the quiet, thoughtful look in Aaron's eyes that he hadn't entirely dismissed her brothers' concerns.

She felt a quick flutter of fear, and had to swallow hard. What Gabe and Yale hinted simply wasn't possible. Bo was good and kind and decent. Maybe he was more charming than most men. But that was just part of his Southern upbringing. As for his choice of living arrangements, that was his business. His and hers.

Cody came dancing up, followed by his little brother. ''Mama said to tell you that supper's ready.''

When the men turned to follow him, Kitty remained beside the corral.

Aaron paused. ''You coming?''

She nodded. ''I'll be along in a minute, Aaron.''

When she was alone she stared at the distant hills, trying to wrap her mind around the things her brothers had told her. When she'd first met Bo, she'd thought of him as a man of mystery. Still, it didn't seem possible that he could be living a life of deception, and hiding behind another man's good name. But though she struggled to put it out of her mind, the seed had been planted. A seed that threatened to take over all the beauty of this long-anticipated day with her family.

Oh, why couldn't things just be simple? Why did they always have to get complicated?

With a huff of despair she turned and made her way to the cabin.

Inside the air was perfumed with all manner of fine foods. The scarred wooden table groaned under the feast Bo and the women had prepared.

Gabe and Yale carried in the chair and bench from the porch and positioned them on either side of the table. Billie and Cara were setting out platters of potatoes and vegetables and baskets of rolls and bread.

Bo had rolled his sleeves and was busy carving thick slices of venison so tender it nearly fell off the bone.

Billie paused beside him and breathed in deeply. "Oh, that smells heavenly, Bo."

He gave her one of those devilish smiles that made her blush before she turned away.

From her place by the door Kitty watched. How

could any man be that charming without any seeming effort? Again her brothers' warnings echoed in her mind and she felt her despair deepen. Was it all an act to lull her and her family into trusting him? But why? What could he possibly hope to gain? This isolated shack offered him nothing of value, except a place to hide. And if he should choose to leave, the only harm done would be to her heart.

She couldn't help placing a hand over the spot. Her poor, trusting heart.

The thought had all the blood draining from her head. For the space of a second she was forced to lean weakly against the door. She didn't think she could bear it if she found out that he'd used her, and lied to her, for his own pleasure.

Seeing her, Bo hurried over and laid a hand gently on her shoulder. "What is it, Kitty?"

"Nothing." She stepped away, avoiding his touch. "It's just a little warm in here."

"I guess it is." He smiled and indicated an empty chair beside Aaron. "Go ahead and sit down so the others can start supper."

"Here, Bo." Billie patted the bench that she and Cara were sharing. "There's room for you between us."

As he took his seat he remarked, "A thorn between two roses."

Both young women blushed and laughed, which

only added to Kitty's annoyance. Could she possibly be jealous? she wondered. Of her own sisters-in-law?

She dismissed the thought at once. It wasn't jealousy she was feeling. It was a deep and abiding anguish. Bo and all that charm set her teeth on edge. All through the interminable meal, her anger grew as she watched the way he managed to charm everyone without any effort.

"Where's your home, Bo?" Cara began cutting the meat on her son's plate.

"Now it's wherever I happen to land. But I was born in Virginia." Bo buttered a roll and popped it into his mouth before turning to Billie with a smile. "These are fine biscuits, ma'am. Much better than mine. Did you use lard?"

"Butter. And I brushed more butter over the crust while they were browning."

He arched a brow. "I hadn't thought of that. I'll give it a try tomorrow."

Gabe cleared his throat. "You don't think of cooking as woman's work?"

Bo shrugged. "Not at all. I enjoy it. All the men in my family liked to cook."

"You have any brothers or sisters?" Yale accepted a platter from his wife's hands and passed it on.

"No. I was an only child. According to my father,

I was lucky to even be born. My mother was frail. But she managed to hang on long enough to see me grown. For that I'm grateful.''

"Did you take care of her, Bo?'' Cara glanced at her two boys, knowing they were listening with avid interest. They had buried their own father more than two years earlier.

"My father insisted on caring for her himself. He bathed her, dressed her, fed her. When she was gone, he buried his grief in work. But he was never the same after that. I knew he was just biding his time until he could join her.''

Billie shook her head, sending wild red curls dancing. "How grand to have had parents who loved each other that much.''

Bo nodded. "I consider myself one of the luckiest people in the world.''

"Why'd you leave Virginia?'' Cody asked.

Bo turned to the boy. "With my father gone, I had no family left.'' His voice lowered. "You're lucky to have a brother. That's a really special bond that nobody can ever break. Even if the two of you disagree, or get so angry you come to blows, you'll find a way to mend things and get back together. That's what brothers and sisters do for one another. They offer wise counsel. And sometimes they have to say some pretty harsh things. But they always look out for each other, in good times and bad.''

Out of the corner of her eye Kitty saw her brothers flush and look away. Gabe and Yale had spent a lifetime fighting, and there had been a time when she had feared that they would never be able to repair the rift. But now that Yale had returned to Misery with a wife and sons, his old days of drinking and gambling had been put away, and he and Gabe had become the best of friends again, much to her relief.

Little Seth's voice lifted in curiosity. "You mean if you had a brother, you'd still be living in Virginia?"

Bo laughed. "Probably. But since I had no family left, I decided to just take off across the country and see where my journey would take me."

"Have you seen the whole country?" Seth asked timidly.

"Not all of it. But I've seen a good bit. I've seen oceans and mountains and cities big and small."

"Why'd you come to Misery?" Cody asked.

Bo saw the way everyone was watching and listening. He smiled at Billie as she filled his cup and moved on, circling the table with the pot of coffee.

"I'd heard about the Badlands. About the rock formations, and the Black Hills, and the uninhabited land that stretched on for hundreds of miles. But what most interested me was what I'd heard about vast herds of mustangs that roamed wild and free.

Being a horseman, I knew I had to see them for myself.'' He idly rubbed the wound at his shoulder. ''Of course, I didn't expect to be greeted by a band of outlaws. But if they hadn't shot me and left me for dead, I'd have never had the opportunity to meet all you fine people.''

Cara moved around the table passing out dishes of custard.

Little Seth dug into his dessert before asking, ''Where will you go when you leave here?''

Over the rim of his cup Bo smiled at Kitty. ''I haven't given that any thought, Seth. Where would you go if you ever left Misery?''

Without hesitation the boy said, ''I'm never leaving Misery. It's the best place in the whole world.''

Bo set down his cup and grinned. ''You're doubly lucky, Seth. You not only have a brother, but you already know what some people don't learn in a lifetime.''

''What's that?'' the boy asked innocently.

Bo winked. ''There's no place like home.'' He glanced over at Aaron. ''How's that custard?''

The old man polished off his second helping and sat back with a sigh of contentment. ''I don't know when I've tasted a finer meal. If we did this every day, I'd get too big to fit through the doorway.''

Billie topped off his coffee and patted his shoulder. "We can't do it every day. But I don't see why we can't make it out here most Sundays."

Aaron beamed his pleasure. "That would surely please me. And I know Kitty would enjoy the company, too." He glanced at Kitty, who had been unusually quiet throughout the meal. "I think this calls for a nip of whiskey, and one of those fine cigars Bo brought me from town. What do you boys say we go out on the porch and leave the ladies alone in here to have a visit?"

While Seth and Cody held the door, the men carried the bench and chairs outside. Billie set the bottle of whiskey and four tumblers on a tray and carried it to the porch, with Aaron trailing slowly behind.

From her position at the table, Kitty watched in silence. It occurred to her that, though Bo had seemed relaxed enough while answering their questions, he'd deftly turned the talk to other things at the first opportunity. Like what Billie did to her rolls. As if he needed any advice on cooking. Or where Seth would go if he ever left Misery. Oh, he was slick, all right.

How could she claim to love a man, and still harbor doubts about his character? What if this wasn't love at all, but one of those foolish female flirtations?

Hadn't Aaron tried to warn her? He'd even gone so far as to extract a promise from Bo that he wouldn't lead her on. But as always, she'd treated Aaron's honest concern with disdain, and had forced herself on Bo.

She had no one to blame but herself if he broke her heart.

Her heart. Her poor aching heart.

For one quick moment she actually thought about sharing her story with Billie and Cara, and asking their advice. Then she imagined herself having to endure a hundred different questions, some of them so personal she wouldn't even have words to frame the proper reply.

She pushed away from the table and stormed across the room, staring at the flames on the hearth. She found herself wishing she were out in the Badlands right now, hot on the trail of a herd of mustangs. Then she wouldn't have to deal with her brothers' suspicions, and Aaron's fear for her, and her own doubts, that were crowding out all the happiness of this day.

"Kitty?" Billie's voice broke through her musings. "Would you rather wash or dry?"

"I'll dry." She crossed the room and picked up a clean linen cloth, idly noting that Bo had washed it along with their clothes the day before.

Without thinking she lifted it to her face and breathed it in. This cabin and everything in it now smelled of him. He had slowly insinuated himself into every part of her life, even down to the smallest detail.

Beside her Billie dipped her hands into the soapy water and gave a sigh of approval. "I swear, since Bo came here, this old cabin sparkles and gleams."

Her words were the final straw. While the two women watched helplessly, Kitty did something she'd never done before.

She burst into tears and began sobbing her heart out.

Chapter Nineteen

"Here, now. What in the world…?" Billie cast a helpless look at Cara, who turned away from the table to gather Kitty into her arms.

"What's happened, Kitty?"

Mortified, Kitty shook her head as fresh tears spilled from her eyes. "I can't talk about it."

"You need to." Billie brushed a hand over her hair, much as she would a child. "Maybe we can help."

"Nobody can help me. I've been so foolish. And now…now…" Kitty sniffed, struggling to put a stop to this humiliating flood.

Cara led her toward a kitchen chair. When Kitty was seated, the two young women knelt on the floor at her feet, taking hold of her hands as they did.

"Now," Billie said gently. "What did you do that you think is so foolish?"

"I…" Her lower lip trembled and she avoided their eyes. "I've been…you know…with Bo, out in the barn."

There was a long moment of silence as the two exchanged quick looks before studying Kitty, her head bowed, her cheeks flaming.

"You and Bo Chandler?" Cara's smile bloomed. "Well, of course. That explains it."

"Explains what?" Kitty shot her a puzzled look.

"Why he always looks so eager to get back here."

Billie nodded. "I know for a fact that Jack Slade offered Bo a room at the Red Dog the other night. I overheard them talking while I was setting up for lunch. But Bo refused, saying he needed to get back to Aaron's place by dark." She shared a smile with Cara. "And now I know why."

"Oh, Kitty." Cara gave a delighted laugh. "This is just wonderful. Who would have thought that our tough, independent little sister-in-law would ever find herself a handsome charmer like Bo Chandler."

At that, Kitty started crying all over again.

"Oh, my." Cara put a hand to her mouth. "What did I say wrong?"

"Don't you see?" Kitty lifted tearstained eyes to the two of them. "You just said the same thing Gabe and Yale said out at the corral. Why would a handsome, educated man like Bo want to waste his time with the likes of me?''

''Why?'' Billie looked indignant. ''The better question ought to be, why wouldn't he? Have you ever seen yourself in a looking glass, Kitty?''

''What foolishness.'' Kitty tried to draw her hand away, but Billie held on firmly.

''Kitty, you're beautiful. And not only that, but you're a fascinating free spirit, as well. Oh, I know there might be some men who'd be afraid of your strength. But not a man like Bo Chandler. Don't you see? He's the perfect man for you. Smart, and so sure of himself, he's not even afraid to tackle cooking or cleaning, or any of the other things most of our men wouldn't dream of doing. That takes a very strong man, indeed.''

Kitty was already shaking her head, refusing to listen. ''Gabe and Yale think Bo's just a handsome drifter, out to take advantage of Aaron and me.''

''Is that so?'' Billie was already on her feet. ''Spoken like older brothers, wouldn't you say, Cara?''

Her sister-in-law nodded. ''It's as plain as daylight. They're jealous.''

''Jealous? Of Bo?''

Cara glanced at Billie for confirmation. ''Until now, they were the only men in your life. It's hard for big brothers to see their little sister as a woman.

And even harder to see her involved with a man. It's probably hard for Aaron, as well. Does he know?''

Kitty's only answer was the flush that stole over her cheeks.

''I'll bet he was angry, too, wasn't he?''

Kitty thought about that first morning, when Bo had carried her up from the barn. ''He and Bo had words. But after that, they seemed to come to some kind of agreement. Until today, I don't think Aaron had any doubt that Bo and I were happy together. But now, all I can think about is what Gabe and Yale told us. I know it has to be wearing on Aaron's mind, too.''

Billie returned to the dishes with a murderous look in her eyes. ''On the ride back to Misery, my husband and I are going to have a little talk.''

''I'll be talking to Yale, too,'' Cara said. ''As soon as the boys are tucked into bed tonight.''

''I don't want to cause trouble in your marriages.'' Kitty looked alarmed as she picked up the square of linen and, following Billie's lead, began drying the dishes.

''There won't be any trouble,'' Billie muttered, giving a vicious swipe of the rag over a blackened pot. ''Unless your pigheaded brother isn't willing to see the error of his ways.''

To change the subject, Cara touched a hand to Kitty's arm. ''In matters of love, Kitty, you can't listen to others. Not your brothers. Not Aaron. Not even us.''

''Then who should I trust?''

Cara brushed a kiss over her cheek. ''Trust your own heart, Kitty, and you'll never go wrong.''

Trust your own heart.

Long after her family had taken their leave, and Aaron had said his good-nights, Kitty paced back and forth in front of the fire, pausing now and then to stare into the flames. She knew Bo was waiting for her in the barn. He'd whispered as much before strolling away more than an hour ago. But still she lingered, playing over and over in her mind all that she'd heard this day.

It was all well and good for Billie and Cara to make light of her brothers' criticism of Bo. But Gabe and Yale were so much more to her than just brothers. They had been father and mother, confidante and best friend to a lost, lonely little girl. Maybe they'd drifted apart in these past years, as their lives took new twists and turns, and family obligations. But their opinion was still important to her. And their suspicions of Bo had left her faith in him badly shaken.

He'd had to notice their cool reception. And yet he seemed oddly unaffected by it. She paused in her pacing. Not only unaffected, but downright accepting of it. As if he somehow understood that Gabe and Yale saw him as an enemy. She folded her hands behind her back, peering intently at the fire, as if hoping to find her answer there in the red-hot coals.

What had he said to young Seth and Cody at the table?

You're lucky to have a brother. That's a really special bond that nobody can ever break. Even if the two of you disagree, or get so angry you come to blows, you'll find a way to mend things and get back together. That's what brothers and sisters do for one another. They offer wise counsel. And sometimes they have to say some pretty harsh things. But they always look out for each other, in good times and bad.

Had he intended those words for Seth and Cody, or had they actually been meant for her? He was so smart. He had that uncanny ability to watch and listen. Had he somehow surmised that her brothers were unhappy with these feelings she had for him?

She crossed her arms over her chest and closed her eyes, almost swaying as the truth dawned. He'd been letting her know that she needn't feel guilty for feeling disloyal to her brothers, or to him. That whatever choice she made, it would be all right with him.

It was one more reason why she loved him so.

Love.

At the sudden realization she went perfectly still.

It was true. She loved Bo Chandler. Loved him as
much as she loved Gabe or Yale or Aaron. Even
more, if truth be told. In his arms she'd found the
kind of contentment she'd never dreamed possible.
He never asked her to be what she wasn't. Never
suggested she ought to learn to cook or clean the
cabin. Never seemed to mind the fact that she wore
buckskins instead of gowns. And seemed genuinely
proud of the fact that she could track a herd and
break a horse to saddle better than he could.

He wasn't like any other man she'd ever known.
He didn't lord his superior strength over her. And
even though he had all that book learning, he never
acted as though he knew more than she did. They
simply knew different kinds of things. Hadn't he told
her as much?

She found herself smiling as she started toward
the door, with Cara's wise advice ringing in her
mind.

Trust your heart, and you'll never go wrong.

Bo finished nailing the last rails of the new stall
in place. As he set the hammer aside, he wiped a
sleeve over his sweating forehead and glanced for
the hundredth time at the barn door.

She wasn't coming.

He'd known, of course, that her brothers had said
something that had her riled. He'd read it in those

stormy eyes the minute she'd come up from the corral this afternoon. Maybe it was the fact that he was an outsider. Or the fact that he had no interest in ranching. Or it could simply be that they would express the same mistrust of any man who courted their sister.

Courted. He nearly laughed aloud at the word. In his home in Virginia, courting had some rigid guidelines. There would be endless dinners in the home of the young lady. All of them attended by every aunt, uncle and cousin in the vicinity. There would be parties given in honor of the young couple, where they could dance and mingle with other young people. The parents would meet, ask pointed questions, and withhold their approval until they were satisfied that it was in the best interest of everyone for the two to wed. It was all very civilized and sensible. And tedious, he thought with a grin.

There was nothing tedious about his pursuit of Kitty Conover. It had happened so quickly, he was still reeling from it. But then, everything about Kitty was so unlike anything he'd ever known in his former life, he had no basis for comparison.

She quite simply took his breath away. The way she looked, like a goddess in buckskins. The way she lived her life, in a manner so fearless, so completely free of restraint, he was filled with admiration. In truth, he was wildly, desperately in love with her. And if she didn't soon come to him, he didn't know what he'd do. Die, perhaps. Or storm the cabin and carry her out here by force.

When the barn door suddenly opened he found himself, as always, staring in amazement at the sight of her. She was the most magnificent woman he'd ever seen, with that cloud of golden hair, and that lean, willowy body encased in buckskins.

She had a way of walking that always did strange things to his heart. It probably came from her years of stalking wild creatures. A slow, steady, silent gait that kept her body rigid, her eyes focused straight ahead.

At the moment they were focused completely on him.

As she walked up to him, he absorbed the familiar jolt.

"I was afraid you might already be asleep in your loft, Kitty."

"And miss having you tuck me in?" She paused inches from him and gave him a smile that had his throat going dry. Then she wrapped her arms around his neck and brushed her mouth over his. "Umm," she whispered against his lips. "This is what I've been wanting."

A kick from the plow horse would have been less potent. He dragged her close and savaged her mouth until they were both gasping.

"I've been missing you." He tugged the buckskin shirt over her head at the same time that she began tearing at the buttons of his shirt.

"Not nearly as much as I've been missing you."

"What kept you?" His mouth was already on hers, with a hunger that had him greedy.

"Maybe I just wanted to test your patience."

"Woman." His hands were in her hair, his mouth causing the most amazing sensations as he ran hot, wet kisses down the smooth curve of her throat. "I have no patience left. I need you. Now."

Though his bedroll was just a few feet away, it seemed entirely too far at the moment. With moans of pleasure and sighs of impatience, they came together in a storm of passion.

Kitty awoke and snuggled into the warmth beside her. But when she reached a hand toward Bo, she found the place beside her in the bedroll empty.

Alarmed, she sat up. In the hazy light of early morning she could see him shaving. When he caught sight of her in the looking glass, he smiled.

"Good morning, sleepyhead."

"'Morning." She rubbed her eyes. "What are you doing up so early?"

"I'm heading into town. I promised Eli Moffat I'd drop by his stables and take a look at some documents for him."

"Don't go into town today, Bo. Stay here with me."

He wiped the soap from his chin before crossing to her and dropping down beside the bedroll. "You're making it pretty tough for me to refuse."

"I'll make it even tougher." She wrapped her arms around him and drew him down, kissing him until they were both forced to come up for air.

He held her a little away and stared into her eyes. "For a female who never did this before, you're certainly a fast learner."

"Oh, I've learned all kinds of things from you, Bo Chandler. And I'd be pleased to show you all of them if you'll just come join me in this bedroll."

"Umm." He kissed her long and slow and deep, and stretched out beside her, running his hand along her spine. "That's the most tempting offer I've ever had, ma'am." He lifted his head and kissed the tip of her nose. "But I've really got to get going if I want to get back from Misery before dark."

"Don't go." Her voice was a little too shrill as he started to get to his knees.

He turned to look at her for a long, silent moment. When he finally spoke, his tone was gentle. "What's wrong, Kitty?"

"Nothing." Because she'd never been able to lie, she knew her cheeks were beet red, but she was determined to bluff. "I just want you here with me."

"Uh-huh." He continued studying her. "I'm sure Aaron will be pleased if we spend the entire day in my bedroll in the barn."

"This isn't about Aaron."

"No. It isn't. So what is it about?"

"I told you. I just want…"

"The truth, Kitty." His tone was more abrupt now.

She looked away. Then with a sigh, she blurted out what her brothers had told her. When she was finished, she watched as Bo stood up and turned away.

Frightened, she scrambled to her feet and grabbed his arm. When he turned toward her she could see the look of fury in his eyes.

"Are you mad at me, Bo?"

"At you?" He shook his head, his eyes narrowing in thought. "This isn't about you, Kitty. It's about me and this stranger who's using my name. Don't you see? He has to be one of the outlaws who shot me."

"But why…?"

He held up a hand to silence her question. "I've never told anyone my full name. The only ones who would know that are the ones who stole my papers from my pocket after they shot me."

He dressed quickly, then reached for his gun belt.

Seeing it, Kitty clutched his arm. "You can't go after them yourself, Bo."

"They're claiming my good name, Kitty. I want it back."

While he saddled his horse, Kitty pulled on her buckskins, determined to go with him. But when she reached for her own saddle he stopped her.

"This is my fight. You stay here with Aaron."

"I'm good with a gun."

"And you think I might not be?"

She couldn't answer that. Instead she squeezed his hand between both of his and looked up into his eyes. "Promise me one thing."

He sighed.

When he didn't refuse she pressed on. "Just promise me that you'll let Gabe do his job as sheriff first, before you do anything on your own."

He managed a grim smile as he touched a hand to her cheek. "All right. I promise. Now I'm going alone. With any luck, I'll be back before dark."

He pulled himself into the saddle and nudged his horse into a gallop.

Kitty raced to the door of the barn and watched until horse and rider disappeared over a ridge. Then, her heart pounding, she leaned weakly against the door, wondering how she could remain here while Bo could be walking right into a nest of rattlesnakes.

Chapter Twenty

By the time Bo reached Misery, his temper had heated to a boiling point, and threatened to spill over and burn whoever got in his way. It went up a notch when he saw Yale and Gabe Conover just walking into the sheriff's office at the end of the dusty main street.

He nudged his horse into a run. At the hitching post he was out of the saddle and inside the office in quick strides. Both men turned, aware of the fire in his eyes.

"'Morning, Bo." Gabe stood beside his desk, his badge winking in the morning sunlight. "You here on law business?"

"I'm here to find out why the two of you didn't bother to tell me someone was using my name."

"Now hold on." Yale, always quick to anger, stepped closer, catching Bo by the front of his lapels.

"The man claimed to be Beauregard Chandler, and had the bank draught to prove it. Why shouldn't we believe him?"

The look in Bo's eyes was enough to make him release his hold and take a quick step back. The tone of his voice revealed the depth of his fury. "Because he's a liar. But more important than that is the fact that you see me here in your town every day, helping your citizens. The least you could have done was come to me with what you suspected."

"What we suspect," Gabe said angrily, "is that a smart con man has found the perfect way to ply his considerable Southern charm on a frail old man and an innocent girl."

"If Aaron heard you call him frail, he'd tan both your hides. As for your sister," Bo's voice softened, "you're right. She is innocent. And wild and impetuous and thankfully she's unconcerned about what others think of her."

Hearing such honesty from this man's lips had both brothers standing with jaws dropped and eyes wide with disbelief.

His tone hardened once more. "But she does care what you two think of her. Whether you like it or not, you're special to her. I'd hate to be the one to come between that kind of family feeling, but right now I'm fighting for my good name, and for the woman I love. And if I have to take on the two of you, I will.''

''Hold on, there.'' Gabe pinned Bo with a look. ''You…love Kitty?''

''You heard right.''

Gabe shot a quick look at his brother, and thought about the tongue-lashing he'd had at Billie's hands the night before. From the look on Yale's face, his Cara had had plenty to say on the subject of his sister and this man, as well.

Yale studied Bo more carefully. ''Maybe we were wrong about you.''

''Maybe. But that's not important right now.'' Bo turned to Gabe. ''I'm sure by now you've gone through your Wanted posters, looking for my face.''

Gabe nodded.

''And you failed to find one with my name on it.''

Gabe's mouth tightened. ''That's right. But new ones come in every week on the stage.''

''Maybe so. Right now I want you to go through those posters again. This time with Yale looking over your shoulder. With any luck, he'll spot the man who claimed to be me.''

The two brothers exchanged another surprised look. Gabe cleared his throat. ''I…never thought of that. I suppose we could do it now.''

Bo gave a quick nod of his head and turned on his heel. "You can find me at Swensen's."

Even before he was out the door, he had the satisfaction of seeing Gabe and Yale settling down at Gabe's desk, preparing to pore over a drawer filled with Wanted posters.

Bo made his way to Swensen's. Milling about inside were the usual ranchers in town for supplies, and a steady stream of housewives and assorted children, as well as a number of strangers. He looked them over carefully, before making his way to the counter, where Inga Swensen was tallying purchases.

As soon as she spotted him, she greeted him warmly. "Bo Chandler. I'm so glad you're in town today. The stage came through yesterday, and there's some mail for you. One envelope is marked important, open immediately."

"Thanks, Inga." He waited while she retrieved several envelopes.

As Bo stood sorting through his mail Inga noticed the way several women both young and old paused to study him with a sigh. Even a grizzled old cowboy who was examining a pair of boots looked him over with interest.

She stepped closer. "Where is Kitty today, Bo?"

Distracted, he barely looked up from his mail. "She's at the ranch with Aaron."

"Will you be bringing her into town for Sunday services?"

He shrugged. "If she wants to come." He tried to imagine Kitty in her buckskins, surrounded by everyone in their Sunday best, sitting through a morning of sermons and hymns. The thought had his lips curving in a smile. Just then he looked up to see Gabe and Yale striding through the doorway. The crowd parted to make way for them.

"Bo. You were right." Gabe drew Bo away from the counter and muttered, "Yale recognized the stranger on a poster that identified him as Eustace Dudley. Part of a gang of train robbers suspected of hiding out in the Badlands."

Yale shook his head. "I feel like such a fool, Bo. I guess I'm losing my touch. In my gambling days, I used to pride myself on being able to tell a good man from a phony before the first cards were dealt."

"No harm done." Bo managed a smile. "At least you weren't fool enough to cash that bank draught without asking for some proof from my bank in Virginia."

Yale gave a sigh of relief and stuck out his hand. "I hope you'll give us a chance to start over."

"Yeah." Bo accepted his handshake, then turned

and did the same with Gabe. "I don't blame either of you for trying to protect your little sister."

Gabe looked sheepish. "We've been doing it for a lifetime. It's hard to let go of old habits." He straightened his shoulders. "My deputy, Lars Swensen, and I will make a sweep of the territory, to see if we can find where these outlaws have their hideout. If we're lucky, they might still be there, and we'll be able to arrest them before they try this in some other town."

"Thanks, Gabe. I have to admit, I won't be able to put this to rest until they're behind bars." Bo stuffed the rest of his envelopes into an inside pocket of his coat. "I'd better get over to Eli Moffat's stables and take a look at those documents."

As he walked away Gabe whispered to his brother, "You think he'll tell Kitty about this?"

Yale shrugged. "He strikes me as a man who plays his cards close to his vest. I'm betting he won't say a word until we've had a chance to make amends."

Gabe shot him a surprised glance. "You sound like you're starting to like Bo Chandler."

His brother grinned. "Yeah. Now that I know he's not a liar and a cheat. How about you?"

Gabe chuckled. "He seems like a good man. But I'm still not sure I like him messing with our little sister."

Yale rolled his eyes. "Better not let Kitty hear you say that. Or our wives."

Still laughing, the two brothers went their separate ways.

"What's got into you, girl?" Aaron, sipping muddy coffee, looked up in surprise when Kitty slammed into the cabin.

"Bo's gone to town."

He grinned. "You and he have a lovers' spat?"

"No. It isn't like that, Aaron." She strapped on her gun belt and began checking the bullets in her pistol.

Aaron's eyes narrowed. "What's going on? What's got you so riled?"

"You remember what Gabe and Yale told us yesterday?"

He nodded. It wasn't something he'd soon forget.

"I told Bo."

"You told…"

She held up a hand to stop his protest. "Bo said the only way a man could have known his full name was if he was the coward who'd shot him in the back and stole his papers."

Aaron leaned back, his coffee forgotten. Then, as the words sank in, he slowly nodded. "That makes sense to me."

"And to me. I made him promise to tell all this to Gabe and Yale as soon as he gets to town."

"And that's why you're loading your gun? You really think you'd point that at your own brothers?"

"Of course not. But Bo left here with an eye for vengeance, Aaron. I'm afraid of what he'll do if he should run into this low-down dirty rotten stranger who shot him and stole his name."

"He'll probably do what any man would. Let the scoundrel answer to Bo's gun."

She sighed. "That's what I'm afraid of."

"You mean you don't think Bo would stand a chance in a gunfight?"

Kitty looked away quickly, to keep the old man from seeing just how deep her fear was. "I know what I can do with a gun, Aaron. But I've never had the chance to see if Bo can even shoot straight."

He got up slowly, leaning heavily on his cane, and touched a hand to her sleeve. "There are some things a man just doesn't want his woman doing for him, girl. I'd think this would be one of them."

"I can't help it." She drew back, breaking contact. "I love him, Aaron. If he's too dumb to save his own life, I'll have to do it for him."

Love. He'd known, of course, that it would come to this. He just hadn't expected it so soon. And neither had she, he'd wager.

"What if you save his life at the expense of his love?"

She swung away. "I don't know. I'm not smart

enough to have any answers. I only know I can't stay here and do nothing while he's facing danger.''

She bolted out the door and pulled herself into the saddle. Minutes later, as the hoofbeats faded away, silence settled over the cabin.

Aaron gave a long, deep sigh. Then he made his way slowly to the barn and began to hitch the plow horse to the cart.

It was going to be a long day, he thought wearily. But he needed to be in Misery.

He just hoped he wouldn't be required to pick up the pieces of Kitty's broken heart when he got there.

''Thanks for your help, Bo.''

''You're welcome, Eli.''

''You didn't tell me what the charge would be.''

Bo shrugged. ''No charge. All I did was read some documents.''

''And for that I owe you.'' The big man thought a minute. ''Tell you what. From now on, you can have the use of a stall, free of charge, whenever you're in Misery.''

''That's more than fair.'' Bo shook hands with Eli Moffat and started back toward Swensen's, touching a hand to the papers in his pocket.

All in all, he'd say this day was going better than he'd expected. Now if Sheriff Gabe Conover was able to arrest that band of outlaws, he'd be home free.

He heard a voice call his name.

"Beauregard Chandler."

He swung around to see three men standing in the middle of the dusty street, midway between Swensen's and the Red Dog Saloon. All three were holding guns pointed at him. One of them was the grizzled old cowboy he'd seen earlier. The other two were younger and tougher in appearance.

The old cowboy grinned, showing yellow teeth. "You never got a chance to see our faces, but we had a good look at yours the day Eustace here shot you. If he'd known the wound wasn't fatal, he'd have shot you again."

Bo's voice was cold as ice. "Eustace Dudley."

The younger man looked more pleased than alarmed as he glanced at his two friends. "Didn't know my reputation had followed me all this way, did you, boys?" He waved his pistol. "I heard the woman in Swensen's call your name and give you the mail that came in. You have something we want."

"You mean proof of my identity?" Bo shook his head. "Sorry. I don't give that to anybody."

"You don't need to give it." The man's eyes narrowed as he walked closer. "I'll just blow you away and take what I want. And with you dead, nobody'll be the wiser.''

''Except the sheriff, and his brother, and all the people I've met in this town.''

''There are plenty of other towns in the Dakota Territory. By the time the sheriff gets the word out, we'll be long gone. And when we stop in the next town, we'll have your bank account emptied, and we'll be living like those millionaires in San Francisco.'' Eustace Dudley leveled his gun at Bo's chest. ''Now hand it over.''

Bo slipped a hand inside his coat pocket and felt the cold steel of his pistol, grateful that he'd taken the time to hide it there. He didn't like the odds of one against three. But this gun would even the odds a little.

He gave a tight smile. ''With pleasure.''

In her whole life, Kitty had never experienced such gut-wrenching fear. Oh, she'd had her moments, when she'd taken a spill from a mustang, or had found herself facing the wrath of nature. But this was something so alien to her, she couldn't seem to get a handle on it.

She knew that Aaron had been trying to warn her about interfering in Bo's business. After all, what man wanted his woman fighting his battles for him? But this was different. She knew how to handle a gun. And she'd been taking care of herself for a lifetime.

Bo Chandler was different from the hard-edged cowboys who grew up here in the Dakotas. What would he know about bare-knuckle brawling? Or about facing an outlaw's gun? He was a gentleman, who'd probably learned how to load a pistol from reading one of his books.

That was a far cry from looking into an outlaw's eyes and seeing his own death.

She knew she was risking his anger by coming to town. But there was just no way she could stay away. He could be in danger. And if that was the case, she had to be there with him.

As she started along the main street of Misery she saw, up ahead, the familiar figure that never failed to stir her heart. Bo, standing there in the noonday sun, facing three men. Her heart gave a sudden hard thud in her chest as she realized the three men were strangers to her.

And all were holding guns. Guns aimed directly at Bo.

Without a thought to herself she dug in her heels and urged her horse into a run.

Before Bo could reach for his gun he saw Seth and Cody round the corner of Swensen's and race toward him. The sight of them had his heart stopping.

"Hey, Bo," the younger boy shouted.

"Hi, Seth. Cody." He fought to keep his voice level as his mind raced ahead. "I asked Inga Swensen to save a peppermint stick for each of you. Why don't I see you inside in just a minute, after I finish up some business here?"

On a shriek of laughter the boys veered into Swensen's.

Thinking of their safety Bo turned to the outlaws. "Why don't we take this behind the saloon, where there won't be so many witnesses."

Eustace Dudley, obviously the leader, narrowed his eyes. "You thinking of trying something slick, Chandler?"

"I'm thinking about the innocent women and children." Bo nodded toward Swensen's, where several women were just strolling out with baskets on their arms. Seeing the drawn guns, they ducked back inside.

"There's no reason why they should be put in danger."

Eustace Dudley thought about it a moment. "I don't give two hoots about them. Doesn't matter to me how many people get hurt." He waved his pistol. "Just keep those hands where I can see them. If you go for your holster I'll drop you right here and now.''

He nodded toward his two companions. ''Why don't you boys just keep an eye out for anyone who decides to be a hero.''

At his words the two outlaws took up positions facing Swensen's and the Red Dog Saloon, their guns trained on the people who had begun to gather in the doorway to see what was happening.

Dudley raised his voice. ''The first one to go for a gun will be eating bullets. You understand?''

At once people disappeared inside, to peer through windows, while doors were slammed shut.

Bo stood perfectly still, assessing the situation. The people of Misery had a right to hide behind their doors. He didn't want anyone else hurt because of him. And since he couldn't persuade these outlaws to take their fight away from town, there was only one thing to do. He would have to bluff as long as possible, and then take his chances on dropping them before they dropped him.

''You wanted this letter from my bank?'' He reached a hand to his pocket, again feeling the cold steel of his hidden pistol.

Dudley shot him a chilling smile. ''That's right. Now give it to me.''

Just then a horse came racing up the middle of the street, and a buckskin-clad figure hurtled through space, landing with a thud against the startled outlaw.

Bo drew his gun from its holster. Before he could fire Eustace Dudley had disentangled himself from Kitty and drew her up, wrapping an arm firmly around her throat.

In his other hand was his gun. Aimed directly at her temple.

''Well, Chandler.'' His voice was pure venom. ''Looks like the fates are smiling on me today. Look what just landed in my arms. One of those innocent women you were so worried about.'' He cocked the gun, and the sound seemed to echo in the deadly silence of the afternoon. ''Now drop that pistol, or I'll drop this female where she stands.''

Chapter Twenty-One

"Don't listen to him, Bo." Kitty struggled against the arms that held her. But this gunman had at least two hundred pounds of pure muscle, and was determined to use every bit of it against her. "No matter what you do, he's going to shoot me anyway."

"He isn't going to hurt you, Kitty. It's me he wants." Bo's eyes narrowed on the gunman, as he unstrapped his gun belt and tossed it in the dirt. "Now turn the woman loose."

Eustace Dudley threw back his head and roared with laughter. "You don't really think I'm going to let her go running for help, do you?"

"She'll give you her word." He fixed Kitty with a steely look. "Tell him, Kitty. Tell him you'll go quietly into Swensen's with the rest of the people, and let us get on with this business between us."

She shook her head. "I won't. If this mangy, dog-eared, flea-bitten son of a mule is going to shoot you, he'll have to shoot me, too.''

''Damn it, Kitty.'' Bo clenched his teeth on the string of oaths that threatened to erupt. How was he supposed to outwit this outlaw with her in the way? He wasn't afraid for himself. But he was terrified now that he wouldn't be able to save her. And she just kept making things worse. ''I want you out of here.''

''And I'm not leaving without you.''

''Now isn't this sweet, boys?''

The two gunmen roared with laughter as they kept their guns trained on the now empty street.

''But the truth of it is, woman, you and your fancy lover boy aren't going anywhere.'' Dudley tightened his grasp on Kitty's throat until she was prying desperately at his hands, unable to take a breath.

He waved the pistol at Bo. ''Hand me the papers that you got in the mail, Chandler.'' When Bo hesitated he pressed on Kitty's throat until her knees buckled and she turned so pale, he could see that she was close to losing consciousness. ''Or would you like to see this pretty little thing die right here and now? I've killed enough people that one more puny female won't matter one way or another to me. It's your choice. What's more important to you? The woman or your name?''

Without a word Bo reached into his inside coat

pocket. Once again his fingers scraped the gun he'd concealed there. It would have all been so easy. But now he would be risking Kitty's life.

He'd fired a gun enough times that it was second nature to him. But he'd never had such a precious treasure hanging in the balance.

Though he knew it was a terrible gamble, it was all he had. If the shot went even an inch in the wrong direction, he'd risk hitting Kitty instead of the man who was holding her.

Could he dare risk being the one to kill the woman he loved?

Ignoring the gun, he withdrew the bank envelope and held it out to the gunman.

Eustace Dudley reached for it, a smile splitting his lips. "Thanks, Chandler. This is going to make me a very rich man. Now I think, just to make sure we get out of town safely, we'll take this pretty little thing along for company."

"The woman stays with me."

Dudley's smile grew. "You have nothing to say about it, Chandler. I'm the one holding the gun."

As his fingers closed around the envelope Dudley felt Kitty suddenly wrenched from his grasp. At the same moment he heard the sound of a violent gunshot, and looked surprised that his legs were failing him.

As he dropped to the ground, he saw Bo holding

a smoking pistol in his hands while shoving Kitty aside.

"How'd you...?" Dudley's words died on his lips as he fell facedown in the dirt.

"Oh, Bo." Stunned, Kitty started to reach for him.

"Stay down, no matter what happens." Bo thrust her to the ground, then stood over her, hoping to draw the fire of the other two outlaws.

"But I..." She looked up and was startled by the sight of the two guns aimed directly at Bo. No matter which one he shot, the other couldn't miss at this range.

She felt her heart contract at the knowledge that he was about to die. There had to be something she could do to save him.

"Which one of us will it be, Chandler?" The grizzled old outlaw gave a chilling laugh. "You can't get us both with just one shot."

"I can try."

"And my horse can fly." The outlaw took slow, careful aim.

Bo could see the people huddled inside the doorway, watching in shocked silence. In an aside he muttered, "When I fire, I want you to run to Swensen's. And don't look back. Do you hear me?"

"Yes, Bo. I hear you."

"Good." He suddenly spun, taking aim at the second outlaw, and firing one quick shot that seemed unusually loud in his ears. As soon as the outlaw dropped to his knees Bo spun the other way, expecting to feel the old outlaw's bullet. Instead he saw him also dropping to the ground.

He looked down to see that Kitty had snatched the pistol that had fallen from Eustace Dudley's grasp and had fired at the same moment he had.

For the space of several minutes an eerie silence settled over the scene. Then, as the enormity of the situation dawned on those who had been watching from behind doors, the town seemed to explode with shouts and screams and frightened calls of reassurance to one another.

Cowboys and gamblers from the Red Dog, led by Jack Slade, spilled through the swinging doors and stood over the three outlaws, who lay in pools of blood.

Someone had gone for the sheriff, who came riding up the street with his gun drawn.

He stopped, surveying the scene with a look of amazement.

He turned to his sister. ''Did you do this, Kitty?''

She shook her head, still too stunned to speak. When she finally found her voice she whispered, ''I took one of them. Bo took the other two.''

Gabe shook his head. ''That was some shooting, Chandler.''

Bo didn't answer. He was staring at Kitty with a look that had the breath backing up in her lungs.

She put a hand to her throat, feeling again the way she had when Dudley had been choking her. "You're mad at me, aren't you, Bo?" She stepped closer, feeling a sense of alarm. He hadn't moved. Hadn't spoken a single word. "Aaron said you'd be mad if I came. But I couldn't help myself. I was so afraid for you, Bo. And I didn't know if…" She could feel the beginnings of tears, and worried that she'd embarrass herself right here in front of everybody in town. But she had to make him understand. She had to. "I didn't know you could shoot like that, Bo. And I couldn't bear the thought of you facing those outlaws all alone."

He stayed where he was, vaguely aware of the people milling about, whispering behind their hands. But all he could see was Kitty, the way she'd looked in the arms of that gunman, having her breath, and her life, slowly choked off. "So you thought you'd better come to my rescue. Again."

"Yes. I…I didn't mean to meddle, Bo. Really, I didn't. I just wanted to keep you from being shot again. I…couldn't stand seeing you hurt."

By now Yale and Cara had joined the crowd, as well as Gabe's wife, Billie. They stood to one side, watching and listening helplessly as Kitty and Bo faced each other.

When Aaron rumbled up in a horse-drawn cart, he stared at the scene, then climbed stiffly down. Leaning heavily on his cane he walked over to stand beside Kitty.

"You hurt, girl?"

She shook her head, keeping her eyes fixed on Bo.

"You all right, son?"

Bo continued staring at Kitty in silence.

Aaron turned to Gabe. "Somebody want to tell me what happened?"

"Near as I can tell, Bo managed to kill two of those three outlaws, despite Kitty's interference."

"She didn't interfere." At Bo's terse words, everyone turned to study him. He kept his eyes steady on Kitty. "She was the boldest, bravest woman I've ever seen."

She lifted her head a fraction. "Are you saying you're not mad at me?"

"How could I be mad when you were willing to risk your life to save mine?"

"But you acted mad."

"I was afraid."

"No, you weren't. I saw you, Bo. Standing there, facing those outlaws, guns blazing." She touched a hand to her heart. "There wasn't any fear in you."

"Not for myself. For you, Kitty."

She swallowed and took a step toward him. "You were afraid for me?"

He nodded and took a step in her direction. "I thought Eustace Dudley was going to kill you before I could find a way to stop him."

"Oh, Bo. I was never afraid for myself." She reached a hand to his arm. Squeezed. "But if anything had happened to you, I'd have wanted to die right along with you."

"That's the way I felt, too."

Seeing the way the townspeople were watching so avidly, Aaron cleared his throat. "Maybe you two can stay here jawboning all day, but these tired old legs are about to fail me unless you get me into the back of that wagon and haul my tired hide home."

At once Kitty and Bo were beside him, walking with him toward the cart. They helped him into the back, where he lay on a nest of quilts. Gabe and Yale retrieved their horses and tied them to the back of the cart.

Then Bo lifted Kitty up to the seat before turning to Gabe. "If you'd like, I can come into town tomorrow to fill out any papers you might require."

"There's no need." Gabe offered his hand. "Just take Kitty and Aaron home, Bo."

Home. It was such a fine word.

"I will." He turned to Yale. "I was pretty rough on you this morning."

Yale shook his head. "No need to explain. I'd have done the same thing in your place."

The two men shook hands.

Bo pulled himself up beside Kitty and flicked the reins.

As the cart rolled out of town, their shoulders brushed and he felt her tremble.

He glanced over. "You all right?"

She shrugged. "That depends."

"On what?"

"On whether you're staying or moving on." When he didn't respond she found she couldn't breathe. Her heart simply couldn't beat.

After what seemed an eternity he turned his head to meet her steady gaze. "I want to stay. But I don't want things to be the way they were before."

She could feel her heart beginning to break a little. "You don't?"

He shook his head. "It's no good."

"No good?" She couldn't speak over the pain in her heart.

"Not the way it is. I want us to be married. I want you to be a wife to me. I want to be a husband to you. In every way."

"Marriage?" There were those darned tears again. "You want us to marry?"

He nodded. "Are you willing?"

She blinked, and the tears started spilling down

her cheeks. "Of course I am. I just never thought you'd be willing to settle for me. For our poor ranch. For living way out in the middle of nowhere."

"You're all I want, Kitty." He put an arm around her shoulders and drew her close, feeling the dampness of her tears on his shirt. "As for your poor ranch…" He cleared his throat. "Maybe we can change that."

"I suppose. With enough hard work."

His voice was tinged with humor. "Well. Hard work and enough money."

"I'll find another herd. And I'll even start raising those disgusting pigs. Jeb Simmons isn't the only one who can be a wealthy pig farmer."

He was fighting now to keep the laughter from his voice. "Kitty, I don't know how to tell you this. You don't have to raise pigs. Or even hunt mustangs, unless that's what you want. I'm…not poor."

"You're not?"

He shook his head. "In fact, I'm a very rich man."

"You are?" She drew a little away to stare up at him.

"Yeah." He drew her close again and said against her temple, "I hope you won't hold that against me."

"I'll…try not to." She buried her lips in his throat, and wondered at the feelings that had bubbled to the surface, making her want to laugh and shout and cheer to the Black Hills in the distance.

In the back of the cart, Aaron closed his eyes and grinned. Who'd have believed that an old man like him could live long enough for something like this?

From the front of the cart came the sound of Kitty's voice. "How'd you learn to shoot like that, Bo?"

Bo's tone was low with humor. "I did a bit of hunting in Virginia."

"More than a bit, from what I saw."

His voice rumbled with laughter. "Are you thinking I might be trusted with a gun now?"

"I'd trust you with anything, Bo. Even with my heart."

"Does that mean you'll marry me?"

"I guess that's what it means."

"Good. Now let's get home."

In the back of the cart, Aaron gave a deep sigh. Darned if he wasn't about to see all three of his lost lambs settled for good.

Life just didn't get any better than this.

Epilogue

"I never thought I'd see this day." Gabe stood on the front porch of Aaron's cabin and watched the arrival of wagons and carts as the townspeople of Misery arrived for the wedding of Kitty Conover to Bo Chandler.

"I never thought I'd see this place looking so fine." Yale held a match to the tip of an expensive cigar. Bo had ordered an entire box of them, to pass around to the wedding guests, along with a case of the best whiskey.

Gabe nodded and paused to admire the view. With an infusion of cash, the north pasture was dotted with corrals, all filled with a mix of mustangs and Thoroughbreds, brought from Virginia. Kitty was having the time of her life surrounded by her beloved horses. Bo had hired three of Jesse Cutler's boys to help with the ranch chores, freeing Aaron to sit on his porch and survey his land like royalty.

As Aaron and Bo stepped outside, Kitty's brothers turned.

"How's the groom holding up?" Gabe called out good-naturedly.

Bo shook his head. "I'd rather face a courtroom full of angry judges. And I know Kitty has to be ready to hide out somewhere until this is over. I'm not even sure how all this came about. All we wanted to do was get married. The next thing we knew, it had turned into the biggest event the town of Misery has ever seen."

Gabe and Yale shared a laugh. "It's our wives. They just love weddings. And poor Kitty just got swept along by them. By now, it won't even seem like her wedding, but rather like theirs."

"It's a female thing." Aaron settled himself into the comfortable new chair Bo had ordered for him, and drew happily on his cigar. "I think we should all just have ourselves a glass of whiskey and let the women enjoy themselves."

Bo produced a bottle and four tumblers, and handed drinks around.

"Here's to the Dakota Territory attaining statehood. I hear it'll be soon," Gabe added. "They've already approached me about becoming a federal marshal."

Yale glanced at Bo. "Did you have a hand in this?

I've heard rumors that you might be the first governor.''

Bo merely chuckled. ''I'm not interested in politics. I'm just happy to be a gentleman rancher and a backwoods lawyer.''

''I think that's what Mr. Lincoln said,'' Aaron muttered. He lifted his tumbler. ''I say we drink to the bride and groom.''

They lifted their glasses and drained them. As Bo was about to refill them he heard the rustle of paper in his pocket and paused. ''I almost forgot my surprise.''

''Surprise?'' Aaron glanced over.

''It's a wedding gift for Kitty. But it's actually for her whole family.'' He got to his feet. ''I'd like to give it to her before the ceremony. Come on.''

Without another word he led the way inside the cabin, with the others following expectantly.

''What's that?'' Fresh from the bubble bath forced on her by Billie and Cara, Kitty stood in the brand-new bedroom that had been added to Aaron's little cabin. A bedroom now crowded with feminine frills that covered every inch of the bed and even spilled over onto the chair in the corner.

Billie held up the white lace gown. ''This was your ma's. You gave it to me when I married Gabe.

And now I'm giving it back to you. It's yours, Kitty.''

Kitty was already shaking her head. ''I can't wear that. I'd feel like the biggest kind of fool. Not to mention what I'd look like.''

''You'd look beautiful.'' Billie turned to Cara. ''Tell her.''

''It's true.'' Cara held up the delicate chemise she'd ordered from a mail-order catalog at Swensen's. ''Now let's get you into this and you'll see for yourself.''

The two women felt as though they had a wildcat by the tail. It took the two of them to hold Kitty down long enough to get her into not only the chemise, but the pantaloons, the petticoat, and finally the long lacy gown.

While Billie fastened the row of tiny mother-of-pearl buttons, Cara stood behind her, fussing with the waist-length golden curls that refused to be tamed.

When they were finished they stood aside so Kitty could see herself in the tall looking glass that Bo had had shipped all the way from St. Louis.

Billie and Cara were practically in ecstasy over the transformation in their sister-in-law. As for Kitty, she studied her reflection with a look of disgust.

''If this isn't the silliest...'' She looked up at a knock on the door, relieved for the interruption.

Billie opened it to admit Gabe and Yale, who were grinning like fools. But one look at their little sister, and the smiles were wiped from their faces.

"Just look at you." Gabe stared at her and felt a lump in his throat. "Oh, Kitty. You look just like Ma."

"I do?"

He nodded. "I know you were too young to remember, but that's exactly how she looked." He turned to Yale. "Don't you agree?"

Yale was staring at her in openmouthed surprise, cursing the sunlight that was burning his eyes. It had to be sunlight. He would never weep over something as simple as his sister in his mother's wedding gown. "Gabe's right, Kitty. You're just like her."

Kitty turned back to study her reflection again. "I wish I could remember her. Or Pa." In the looking glass she caught sight of Aaron and turned to fly into his arms.

For the space of a minute he just held her. Then he drew her a little away with a sigh. "Look at you, girl. You're just about the prettiest thing I've ever seen."

"You don't think I look silly, Aaron?"

"Silly? What kind of nonsense is that?"

"You see?" Billie walked up behind Kitty and fastened the gauzy veil to her hair. "Cara and I tried to tell her she looked perfect. But she just didn't want to believe us." She turned to Kitty. "Now do you believe?"

"Not until I hear it from Bo." She saw him standing in the doorway and felt her heart give a quick little hitch.

Would it always be this way? she wondered. Would he always have the power to touch her with a single look?

"Do I look silly, Bo?"

He felt, for a moment, as though he'd lost his voice. In truth, she looked like a fragile angel, spun out of glass.

Then recovering quickly, he shook his head. "You couldn't look silly if you tried. You'll always be the most beautiful woman in the world to me, Kitty."

When he felt his world settle, he reached into his pocket and removed the envelope. "I brought you a wedding present."

"You did?"

He opened the envelope and withdrew a document. Glancing around at the others he explained, "My father still has many friends in Washington. I decided to call in a few favors. After Kitty told me the story of your father, I decided to do a little investigating. A retired judge, who was an old friend of the family, has been able to confirm that Clay Conover had indeed been given a secret assignment by President Lincoln to assume the role of an outlaw in order to infiltrate the many bands of outlaws taking refuge in the Badlands. As you know, the immediate months after the assassination of President Lincoln were pretty chaotic, and many records were either lost or destroyed. According to this letter, your father was able to document many of the most famous outlaws of his day, at great risk to his own life. By the time he had completed his assignment, his health was failing. He returned to his father's farm, only to learn that his wife and children were gone. He died, never knowing how to reach you. But he left this legacy behind.''

Bo unfolded the document and read, ''For his unselfish service to his fellow man, the Government of the United States owes a debt of gratitude to Clay Conover. Because of his courage in the face of danger, his name shall be honored forever by his fellow Americans in the hallowed halls of the government he served so faithfully.''

He handed over the document and watched as Kitty, Gabe and Yale touched it almost reverently.

Gabe struggled to clear his throat. ''After hearing that my father was an outlaw, I became a lawman. I suppose I was attempting to atone for his sins.''

Yale nodded before finding his voice. ''And it was because of what I believed about my father that I became angry and defiant.''

Kitty studied her two brothers through a mist of tears. ''I don't remember him. But I've always thought of him as lost to me.'' She turned to Bo, her lips trembling. ''And now I have my father back. Oh, Bo. What a wonderful gift you've given me. Given all of us. I'll never forget it.''

''Well.'' Moved beyond words, Aaron waved a hand toward the door. ''I think it's time we gave these two a minute to themselves.''

''Only a minute,'' Cara whispered as she brushed a kiss over Kitty's cheek. ''The preacher is waiting.''

''We'll be right outside with your flowers,'' Billie murmured as she caught Gabe's hand and led him from the room.

When the door had closed behind her family, Kitty smiled shyly at Bo. ''This is such an amazing gift. I don't have anything fine to give you in return.''

''You've given me the finest gift of all, Kitty. I was all alone in the world. And now I've become part of this big noisy family.''

''You don't mind that there are so many of us?''

He grinned and drew her into the circle of his arms. At once he felt the warmth begin to spread and grow around his heart. ''I hope, before we're through, there will be many more.''

''Oh, yes. Babies.'' Her smile blossomed. ''I

don't know the first thing about them, but I think it might be fun to learn.''

''You're good at learning.''

''Yes, I am.'' She lifted her arms to encircle his neck and brought her lips to his for a long, lazy kiss. ''And you're a very good teacher. And now…'' She drew away and tugged the veil from her head. ''There isn't much time. Give me a hand, Bo.''

''A hand?'' He stood back, watching her with a puzzled look as she began fumbling with the row of tiny buttons.

''With this mangy old flea-bitten thing.'' She peeled away the gown, and stepped out of the filmy undergarments, before reaching for her buckskins. When she was dressed, she studied herself in the looking glass. Suddenly his reflection was there behind hers, his arms around her waist, as he pressed a kiss to the sensitive skin behind her ear.

''You don't mind, do you, Bo?''

''Mind?'' He laughed, then caught her hand and started toward the door. ''Kitty Conover, I love you just the way you are. Promise me you'll never change.''

''I promise.''

''And promise me something else.''

She paused.

''In an hour, slip away and meet me in the barn.''

As the meaning of his words sank in she started laughing. "Don't you think we'll be missed?"

"I don't care." He gave her one of those heart-stopping grins. "I'm not going to wait until this day is over to love you."

She followed him out the door and heard the gasps from her family when they realized what she'd done. But now, with her hair free of the veil, and her lithe young body encased in the familiar buckskins, she felt more at ease. And with Bo beside her she felt complete.

Complete.

That's what he'd done not only for her, but for her brothers, as well. Because of this one special man, they had their good name back. Bo, who'd had to fight to get his own name back, would understand that.

Kitty glanced around as the whole town of Misery stood watching. There were Inga and Olaf, and Doc Honeywell. Jesse Cutler and his whole brood, and Eli Moffat. Amazingly, there was Emma Hardwick, standing right beside Jack Slade. If she didn't know better, Kitty would think they were holding hands.

Then she tore her gaze from everyone.

She would have preferred to be all alone with Bo in a green spring meadow, speaking their vows for only each other. And then she realized the truth.

They would have the rest of their lives together. This day was just one of many.

But oh, what a grand day it had become. What had her mother once promised?

I want you to know that my spirit will always be with you. Don't be afraid. You have your father's blood flowing through you. That Conover blood will make you strong enough to prevail over anything.

"Oh, Mama," Kitty whispered as she took her place in front of the preacher. "You were right. We did prevail. And now I have a man who'll love and cherish me just the way Pa loved and cherished you."

She turned to Bo, shutting out the crowd.

When it came time to promise to obey, she paused and glanced at Bo. He winked and grinned, and she knew, as he did, that it was the one thing she'd never agree to. Nor would he want her to. He'd made his peace with her obstinate nature, her freewheeling lifestyle.

And then she was speaking her vows in a clear, strong voice, promising to love this one man for all time.

For all time.

Not just in this lifetime, she knew. Theirs was a very special love which, like their parents before them, would burn brighter than the sun, and would shine for all eternity.

* * * * *